ONE WAY TICKET

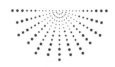

TRICIA O'MALLEY

LOVEWRITE PUBLISHING

ONE WAY TICKET

"If you are not willing to risk the unusual, you will have to settle for the ordinary." – Jim Rohn

CHAPTER ONE

The door was locked.

Paige jiggled the handle, confused, because her boyfriend Horatio subscribed to an open-door policy. This welcoming attitude and willingness to trust others was what had originally drawn Paige to him. Sometimes she felt like his mother, trying to caution Horatio to protect his interests, but he'd just laugh, pat her on the head, and tell her she worried too much. If she pressed an issue, Horatio would pull her to bed and make her forget what had ever bothered her to begin with.

Maddening at times? Sure. But fun? It certainly was. It made the responsibilities that weighed heavily on her shoulders each day seem less of a burden and more a badge of honor. Especially when the other yoga students at the studio gazed her way, envy in their eyes, when Horatio wrapped his arms around Paige and insisted his students defer to her for all their scheduling needs. "In time, my goddess, in time," Horatio would say, soothing her worries away.

Finally finding her key, she unlocked the door and pushed it open, hanging her tote on a hook by the door. The front door opened directly into a small main living area, with a tiny but efficient kitchen done in white on white, tucked to the side. Two doors led from opposite sides of the main living area, each leading to generous sized bedrooms with attached baths. One of the rooms they'd converted into an office and Paige poked her head in there first. A sigh escaped her as she surveyed the mess of papers that had been dropped onto her desk while Horatio's remained immaculate except for his sleek little computer, a bowl of crystals, and a large framed photo of himself in warrior pose. Turning, Paige left the room and opened the door to their shared bedroom.

"Oh my god!" Paige gasped, her hand to her mouth, as she took in the tangle of limbs and…so much nakedness… on her bed. *Their* bed.

"Paige, my goddess, you're home," Horatio smiled to her from where he leaned against the cushioned headboard, one *she'd* picked out, and sliced a sliver of an apple with his ritual knife. He handed the slice of apple to one of the current teachers-in-training, Lily, who was curled at one side. On the other, Nadia, also an instructor in the same class, stretched languidly and smiled at Paige like she'd just inked the deal on a well-padded prenuptial agreement.

Everyone was naked.

"I *am* home. The…the door was locked…" Paige said, feeling stupid as they all stared at her like *she* was the intruder. Nobody made a move to get up or even exhibit any type of chagrin. If anything, Lily looked annoyed at Paige for interrupting.

"It was? That's odd," Horatio mused, stretching his tanned limbs out – a spray tan, at that – and offered a slice of apple to Nadia.

"I locked it, Horatio." Nadia batted her eyelashes up at Horatio while Paige tried to breathe through the murder fantasies currently playing out in her head.

"Now, Nadia, you know that's unacceptable. Having an open-door policy is very important to me," Horatio said, his voice stern, and turned to hand her piece of apple over to Lily instead. Pushing her lush lower lip out, Nadia picked at a wrinkle in the sheet.

"I thought it was for the best."

"I'll have to punish you, as you well know," Horatio sighed, and laid his hand across her bum, spanking Nadia enough to make a small squeak emanate from her perfect doll-like mouth but not enough to leave a mark.

"Excuse me," Paige said, drawing their attention back to her, "but what the hell is going on here?"

"What does it look like?" Lily giggled, winding a leg around Horatio's and smiling up at Paige. It hurt to see them so casually wrapped around Horatio, but Paige couldn't decide if it was because they were younger and bendier, or because Horatio was cheating on her, which probably said something about the current nature of her relationship.

Paige filed that thought away to examine more deeply on another day when she wasn't confronted with a smorgasbord of boobs and butts on her favorite sateen sheets.

"Both of you...out!" Paige ordered, pointing to the

women, and it was a credit to her patience that she didn't grab for Horatio's ritual knife when they both looked to him for guidance instead of listening to Paige's command first.

"You look tense, my goddess. Why don't you join us?" Horatio asked.

"I'm sorry…what?" Paige stood there, mouth hanging open, feeling like she'd walked into a play that she didn't have the script for.

"Join us, please," Horatio said, his blue eyes crinkling at the corner as he smiled at her and patted the bed. "It will relax you."

"You can't be serious," Paige said, heart hammering in her chest, as her world tilted on its axis.

"Please, my goddess, join us. You'll feel wonderful after. I'm certain we can loosen that dark energy in your third chakra. I can feel it from here."

Paige's eyebrows almost hit her hairline.

"My chakras? You're concerned about my chakras right now?"

"Seriously, Paige, we've been meaning to talk to you about them anyway," Lily sniffed, and Paige zeroed in on her.

"I'm sorry…what?" Paige said, feeling like a parrot squawking the only phrase it knew.

"Your chakras. They've become a bit of a problem at the studio."

"It's bringing us all down," Nadia confirmed.

"I think I'm going to take a shower." Lily yawned and reached for a pink robe next to the bed. Paige's pink robe.

She'd saved for weeks for that robe and was pleased when she finally decided to splurge on herself.

"You and you," Paige said, finally jumping into action and grabbing each of the women's arms, "get out!" Pulling them unceremoniously from the bed, she bent and picked up discarded clothes, tossing them into the living room, and shoved the astounded girls from the bedroom before slamming the door in their faces.

"Hey! My iPhone's in there!" Nadia yelled.

Paige turned and locked the door.

"Not feeling like sharing? That's fine. You only had to say so, my goddess. No need to get rough with the girls." Horatio stretched before standing and turning toward the bathroom.

"Nope," Paige said, blocking his path and forcing him to step back until his butt hit the bed again. Looking up at her, he pinched his nose and sighed.

"Paige, I guess it's time I talk to you about this. It's something I should've brought up earlier…"

"*This* being the fact that you're cheating on me?" Paige crossed her arms over her chest and glared down at him. His golden hair was tucked into his usual man-bun and what she'd once thought was cute now looked like a good handle to grab and smash his face into something. Something hard, preferably.

"No, about your chakras… and your attitude. It's really bringing a cloud to the studio," Horatio said and to Paige's shock, he reached out and patted her arm. "I think you need to get some help. I've done what I can, but there's only so much you can work out during yoga. It might be best for you to find a counselor."

"I...what? You're saying this is *my* fault?" Paige's mouth gaped as she pointed from Horatio to the bed.

"There is no blame here," Horatio said, using his soothing yoga voice as though he was trying to calm an unruly dog.

"Yes, Horatio, there *is* blame here. On you, specifically, for cheating on me," Paige enunciated clearly, her body almost vibrating with anger.

"How can there be cheating? I don't cheat. I've always had an open-door policy," Horatio said, shrugging a shoulder and once more reaching out to run a hand down her arm. Paige pulled away from his touch, her mind scrambling as she tried to take in his words.

"Open-door policy to your teachings. To your classes. To your home for rituals or meditation sessions," Paige clarified.

"Yes, for that too."

"But not to your bedroom. *Our* bedroom."

"I never said that."

"Wait...are you telling me that all along..." Paige gulped a breath as her mind flashed back over the past two years. The other students eying her. The whispers. She'd always thought it was because they were envious of her relationship with Horatio. He was a charming man and he'd gathered admirers with ease. Paige had never begrudged any of his students for looking up to him.

"Paige, my goddess, you know I don't believe we're meant to be monogamous."

"I do?" Paige asked, incredulous. She most certainly did *not*.

"Of course. It's too restricting for our carnal nature.

We're meant to come together with others, to enjoy the beauty and union that can come from sharing in physical pleasure together. It's important to our chakras that we remain open and welcoming to all."

"I'm fairly certain our chakras can be healthy without my bed being a revolving door of partners."

"That's coming from a place of judgment, Paige. What did I say about that?"

"Judgment comes from fear," Paige said automatically and then clamped her mouth shut. How easily was this man leading her to his side in this argument? What a fool she'd been.

"Exactly. And we shouldn't judge others on their path. This is my path, Paige. I'm meant to share my love and my expertise with the world. It's what I'm here to do. Don't you see? That's why I'm so at peace with myself." Horatio smiled blissfully up at her, assuming Paige would understand.

"I suspect it's the multiple orgasms that have brought you calm, not some higher calling," Paige bit out.

Horatio recoiled as if slapped. "This is what I mean, Paige. Your attitude...well, it needs adjusting. I've tried, but I think it's best if you seek your help elsewhere. I've done all I can here."

"I'm sorry, what? You're...breaking up with *me*? Even though you are the cheater? And the liar?"

"I never cheated or lied. I've always been honest about having an open-door policy."

"A little clarification on what that meant might have been nice before I moved my entire world into yours!" Paige shouted, hands on her hips, fury raging through her.

No way was he going to deny her the righteous indignation she was due.

"I don't think I could have been any clearer. Open-door is pretty self-explanatory."

Paige's mouth fell open as she struggled for words. Had she been that blind? Was he in the right about this? Or was he just twisting it for his own benefit? Confusion raced through her as she stared down at him.

"You've a good soul, my goddess, but you need more help with clearing your chakras than I can give. It's time for you to move on. Your path will be lighter for it." Horatio nodded as though he was giving her a roadmap to happiness. He was so sold on his own guru status that he couldn't see he was being a condescending prick. Luckily, Paige wasn't so far gone that she couldn't.

"You're a fake," Paige said, and a storm cloud washed over Horatio's face. "A *fake*. A liar. A user. A manipulator. And you'll never get what you want, no matter how much you seek your path, Horatio. I've never seen dirtier chakras in my life."

Not that Paige could see chakras, but she enjoyed the anger that roiled across Horatio's face.

"It's time for you to pack your things and go," Horatio said.

"Oh, trust me, I was on my way."

"Most of your stuff is packed for the retreat anyway. It shouldn't take long. I'm going for a swim in the meantime." Horatio stood, his tall lanky body hovering over hers before he bent to press a kiss to her head. "Be well, my goddess."

CHAPTER TWO

Frozen by what had just happened, Paige didn't even lash out as Horatio tried the door, annoyance flashing over his face when he found it locked. He turned the lock before he strolled out toward the pool. He would swim naked, Paige knew, and now she better understood why he got such a killer deal on this house from their female landlord.

His landlord. She wasn't even on the lease.

Paige railed at herself as she began to pace the room. What an absolute idiot she'd been. She'd let herself get swept away and now she had nothing. No job, no place to go, and no partner to help her. No family, either, for that matter. Which was maybe how she'd landed in this mess, but that was one particular wound she wasn't willing to open today.

"Breathe," Paige repeated to herself, over and over, like a mantra, as she collected her things and dumped them into duffle bags. One bag, already packed for their upcoming retreat to Poco Poco Island, held most of her workout gear. There wasn't much else to add. For years now she'd been carefully saving her meager salary and living as a minimalist out of respect for both the environment and for the restraints of her budget. Now, looking at the two duffle bags and a hastily packed backpack, her stomach did a weird little dance. Was that all there was to her existence in this world?

"The office! Right," Paige said, refocusing on her breath before she did something stupid like taking Nadia's iPhone and smashing it against the wall. Reaching for her favorite sheets, which *she* had purchased, her hand paused as she took in the stains on the bed.

"Ew. Nope, nope, nope. Let them go, Paige." Though it killed her – those sheets had been procured from a sweet online sale at Neiman Marcus – Paige hauled her bags to the main room and stopped by the office to go through the stack of papers. Realizing she didn't need to take the work stuff with her, she paused for a moment and plopped into the chair, staring down at the itinerary for the upcoming three-week retreat on Poco Poco Island.

A tear dripped down her face and landed with a little plop on the glossy brochure that promised a retreat where one could get in touch with their inner yoga goddess. Since her inner goddess was currently contemplating ways to inflict excruciating pain in a slow, measured, and deliberate manner on Horatio, Paige didn't think the retreat was really up to the monumental task of sorting out the current mess of her life. Sighing, Paige buried her face in her hands and forced herself to breathe deeply for a moment before she committed several federal crimes and ended up in prison.

She was fairly certain that a jail cell would wreak havoc on her chakras.

Paige had met Horatio at a particularly vulnerable point in her life – when she'd found herself out of a job and with no family to rely upon – and she'd moved almost effortlessly into Horatio's life. Her own fault, really. Paige swiped the back of her hand across her cheek to stop another tear from dropping onto the brochure. While there had been a gazillion red flags, Paige had studiously ignored them as easily as she ignored the serving size recommendations on a bag of Doritos and had seamlessly moved her way from yoga student to girlfriend, home-maker, and business manager for Yoga Soulone. From day one, Horatio's needs had consumed her, and just like that, they were gone as fast as leaving an unattended bag in the subway.

Her eyes fell on the brochure again. Images of sunny skies, sandy beaches, and pretty striped umbrellas dotted the brochure that guaranteed a relaxing stay at Tranquila Inn on little Poco Poco Island in the Caribbean. Before she could second-guess herself, Paige picked up her phone.

"Tranquila Inn." A woman's voice, with a faint hint of a British accent, answered the phone.

"Yes, hello, this is Paige Lowry from Yoga Soulone in Santa Cruz. I'm calling about our upcoming retreat next week."

"Yes…about that…" the woman said, but Paige cut her off.

"I'm afraid we'll have to cancel the retreat."

"Oh really? Well, that's just silly." Paige pulled the phone back as laughter tinkled through the phone's speaker. "But I suppose that's typical for the day I'm having."

"Oh, I'm sorry to hear that." Paige said, not sure what this woman was going on about.

"Yes, well, these things do happen," the woman agreed.

"I'm sorry…with whom am I speaking?"

"This is CeCe Alderidge, owner of this lovely establishment. And I'm having a bad day."

"Ah, well, that makes two of us," Paige said, pulling out desk drawers to see if she was missing anything to pack.

"Oh really? Do tell! I so love a good story," CeCe insisted.

Paige raised an eyebrow but decided to go for broke. "Well, you see, CeCe, I've been in a relationship with the owner of Yoga Soulone for the last two years, and I run his business for him. I also live with him. Today I came home and found him in bed with two of our yoga trainees."

"Oh dear," CeCe sighed.

"Oh dear, indeed."

"And so now you are canceling the trip? I hope you don't let him take this away from you."

"I *am* canceling the trip. You see, CeCe, he told me my chakras were out of line, that we've always had an open relationship, unbeknownst to me, and then he broke up with me and asked me to pack and leave."

"Well, now, that's just plain churlish."

"Isn't it? I now have no place to live, no job, and no boyfriend. So, yes, it's been a bad day for me as well. What's your story?" Paige couldn't believe she was unloading on this poor woman, but CeCe seemed genuinely interested.

"My events manager quit! Just up and quit, for no reason at all. With a high season full of retreats coming up. Can you imagine?"

"I can imagine that is quite stressful."

"I'm in a right tizzy about it, I am."

Paige heard ice cubes clinking in a glass in the background, as though someone was swirling their cocktail in the air.

"Well, I'm canceling the retreat for Yoga Soulone as they won't have a coordinator to run it while on Poco Poco Island. That should ease some of your immediate stress."

"Wait!" CeCe exclaimed.

"I'm sorry, I just don't see how it would work. I handle everything for Horatio. He's going to realize that once I leave and this retreat will fall apart."

"Forget Horatio. But, what a name, if I do say so myself. Anywho, darling, I'd love it if you'd come work for me."

"Excuse me?" Paige said, pulling the phone away and then putting it back to her ear.

"Yes, yes, this is exactly what's needed. You dropped into my lap at the most prolific of times."

Paige wasn't sure "prolific" was the correct word, but she didn't have time to question CeCe as the woman rattled on.

"*You're* a coordinator. I just lost a coordinator. You know yoga and all that...woo-woo stuff."

"Woo-woo stuff?" Paige raised an eyebrow again. Oh, if only Horatio could hear this woman.

"Oh, please, my dear, don't let me offend you. To each their own and all that. It's how we make our money anyway. Say you'll take it, please."

"Take it…the job, that is? You're offering me an events coordinator job at your hotel?"

"Well, we can't really be called a hotel. Perhaps we are. A small hotel. A boutique hotel!" CeCe exclaimed. "And we'd love to have you come work for us. At least for the high season? See how it goes?"

"But…what about work visas? Residency? Can I just *do* that?"

"Of course, darling. Americans can come for six months at a time before they need residency," CeCe said. "Wait, are you American? Where did you say you were from?"

"From the Yoga Soulone Studio in Santa Cruz, California."

"Of course, lovely to meet you…"

"Paige." Paige almost laughed.

"Paige! Perfect. Darling. *Please*. Help an anguished woman out? I'd be destitute without you."

"Um…"

"Room and board are included, of course. We're right on the water, with a lovely beach. I'm sure you've seen our brochure?"

Paige picked up the glossy brochure on the desk in front of her. Her tear had smudged the lettering on the front. Despite her current turmoil, the sandy beach with its striped umbrellas and colorful hammocks did look incredibly appealing. Or maybe it was because of her current turmoil that it was even more appealing? Hard to say, really. Either way...

"You've got a deal, CeCe. When do you need me?"

"Tomorrow?" CeCe asked and Paige shook her head and laughed.

"I'll see about changing my ticket and email you with my details."

"Perfect! Oh darling, what a serendipitous day it has been. Mariposa! Another martini please..."

Paige stared at the brochure as CeCe clicked off and wondered if she'd lost her damned mind or if, for once, things were actually working out in her favor.

CHAPTER THREE

Paige grabbed the seat in front of her as the plane lurched, dipping on the wind, her stomach dropping with it. She eyed the pilot, who mopped his face with a towel a few seats in front of her. Was he sick? Or was he just sweating this much because it was ungodly hot in this tin-can of an airplane currently hurtling toward a speck of an island in the middle of the Caribbean Sea? Tearing her eyes away from the pilot, she trained her gaze outside the window and focused on the propellers blurring as they moved. That didn't help either, Paige realized, as she eyed the screws holding the wheels of the plane on. It would just take one to pop off and the wheel would plummet to the crystalline water below them.

Gulping a breath, Paige hugged her purse on her lap and wondered again why she'd had to change her flights. Surely, another week couldn't have mattered that much, not when Tranquila Inn was hiring internationally? Instead, she'd rescheduled her flights. Because this was an "off" day to get to Poco Poco Island, apparently, the travel agent had routed Paige through a sister island.

The travel agent had failed to mention she'd be offloaded from her air-conditioned jet to a six-seater prop plane, however. Grateful she'd decided to only bring her one duffle bag, for that was all the weight limit allowed on this small plane, Paige had tucked into her miniscule seat and closed her eyes for takeoff. Even she was surprised when the whirring of the engine threatened to send her to sleep, but that was more likely due to the last two nights of minimal rest. Paige had crashed at her friend Jane's house, who'd kindly offered up her couch for sleeping. With three kids under the age of five, there wasn't much that could be done about noise or sleep, but Paige had been grateful to have a place to stay anyway. Jane had been kind enough to stash the rest of Paige's stuff in their shed out back, and with a quick goodbye, Paige had been off on her adventure.

Another dip in the plane ensured she'd not actually be able to fall asleep – what with the threat of an immediate and painful death and all – and instead Paige worked on her yoga breathing to calm herself.

"Not long now," the man in the seat across from her said, the music of the islands in his voice. "It's only a short flight."

"Thanks," Paige said, biting her lips together.

"Are you on vacation?"

"No, I'm headed to Poco Poco Island to work, actually," Paige smiled.

"Ah, that's nice. It's a small island. I'm certain we'll see you around. Where will you be working?"

"At Tranquila Inn."

The man's eyes widened in his face and he slapped his thigh, letting out a loud laugh, before he nudged the man next to him and spoke quietly to him. His seat partner craned his neck to look at Paige, before shaking his head and murmuring unintelligibly.

"Is that a bad thing?" Paige piped up, eager for more information, grabbing the seat in front of her again as the plane took a particularly large dip.

"I'm sure you'll be fine. There, see? We'll be arriving now." The man pointed out the front window and Paige was distracted by the small landing strip that seemed to be coming at them way too fast. Closing her eyes, she held her breath until they bumped across the tarmac, skidding to a stop much too haphazardly for Paige.

"All right, everyone!" the pilot boomed, startling Paige and the other three people on the flight. "Welcome to Poco Poco Island! If you live here, welcome home. If you're visiting, we hope you enjoy your stay."

"Not if you're working for Tranquila," the man next to her said, and everyone on the plane broke into laughter.

"Wait…what does that mean? What am I getting into?" Paige asked, but by then the pilot had opened the door and put a little stool on the tarmac for people to step down. She was the last off, and by the time she waited for the pilot to hand her the duffle bag he'd stored in the back, the other passengers were gone.

"Sir, is there something wrong with Tranquila Inn?" Paige asked the pilot, who had shaded glasses covering his eyes.

"Not at 'tall, miss. Don't let 'em get to you." With that,

he disappeared to fill out a clipboard and motioned to a few people who waited on the tarmac, their luggage at their feet. It appeared the pilot and his plane would load up, turn around and go back to the other island – like a taxi – and she wondered how often people bounced around the islands that way.

Wiping the sweat from her brow with the back of her hand, Paige pulled her sunglasses from her purse and walked across the boiling hot tarmac toward the customs sign, regretting her choice of jeans. She'd already tied her cardigan around her waist, but there wasn't much else she could do but sweat and wait to get to her new home so she could change out of her long pants. It wasn't worth digging through her pack in the airport bathroom just to feel marginally cooler.

Breezing through customs, as she was the only one in line and the agent wasn't interested in making conversation, Paige walked to the front of the small airport and into the carpark. There, she shaded her eyes and looked around for a woman who would resemble one Ms. CeCe Alderidge. Not that she had any clue what this woman looked like, but she'd painted a picture of a free-wheeling older woman draped in a colorful sarong, or perhaps a wide-brimmed hat.

She never did respond to your email.

That thought had worked its way through Paige's mind more than once on the trip down, but she'd taken it with a grain of salt. Clearly the woman was overwhelmed, and likely managing everything on her own. She'd been very adamant about offering Paige a job and Paige had every faith she'd make good on it. Or was that Horatio's voice in her head? She'd been second-guessing everything he'd taught her over the past couple of years, and one of them was that they were supposed to innately trust the good in people. But how could she trust the good in people when the person teaching her that lesson had lied? Well, in his version of events it wasn't lying, but Paige was not ready to entertain that version even in the slightest.

It pleased her to no end that he'd already started calling, and leaving voicemails with questions about the business. Actually, *only* with questions about the business. She'd ignored every call, and in doing so, slowly took her power back. It would be baby steps for a while since she still felt shaky, but there was nothing like a new adventure to force her to keep moving forward.

Looking around and seeing nobody in particular who looked to be waiting for the occupants of this flight, Paige moved into the shade and cursed her choice of jeans once more. Dropping her pack at her feet, Paige pulled the hair tie from her wrist and bundled her mass of dark hair in a ragged knot on top of her head. Immediate relief greeted her as the breeze tickled the back of her neck, and she leaned against the wall to take in her surroundings.

"Taxi?" A man called to her from where he sat playing dominos at a rickety table on the sidewalk with another man.

"Um, maybe. I thought someone was supposed to pick me up, but now I'm not so sure."

"You let me know."

"Okay," Paige said, sliding her phone from her purse and turning it on. While it searched for data, Paige went back to observing where she'd landed. The parking lot of the airport was small, maybe fitting thirty cars at best, and a ragged road brimming with potholes ran parallel to the airport outside the car park. Across the street was a small food truck, a pebble beach, and the bluest water Paige had ever seen. She immediately wanted to take off her clothes and dive in. The vibrating of her phone in her hand pulled her attention back from the water, and she looked down to see a few emails and text messages show up.

None of which were from Tranquila Inn.

"Sir?" Paige called, picking up her bag and striding to where the men continued their fierce game of dominos.

"You do need a taxi."

"I do."

"Where you headed?"

"I'm going to Tranquila Inn."

"Oh, I can't help you then." The men's eyes met over the domino board.

"What? Why?"

"Can't do it."

"Why not? You just asked if I needed one. Please...I don't have any other option."

"How you payin'?" The man, clad in jeans and a button-down, with not a drop of sweat on his face, leaned back to look at her.

"I can pay."

"Did they say they'd pay?"

"Who? The inn?"

"Yes."

"No, they didn't. I will pay. I have cash."

"Let me see it."

"That's...no, I'm not letting you see my cash. That's

not a smart thing for a woman traveling alone to do," Paige huffed.

"She's right," the other man pointed out.

"Fine, fine. I'll take you. But you give me the cash before you get out or I will drive you right back here."

"Ohhh…kay…" Paige drew that word out. "How much?"

"Thirty."

"Is that the local price or the tourist price?"

"That's your price." The man looked her up and down.

"Listen, I don't have a lot of money and now I have no clue what's going on with my job at Tranquila Inn and I'd really like it if you were fair with me."

"Oh, you're working there? Hmm, okay, I'll do it for twenty. Mainly because you're going to need the money. Unless you talk to Jack. Make sure you talk to Jack. He's good for it."

"Who's Jack?" Paige asked, following the man as he grabbed her duffle bag and put it in the back of a truck before ushering her inside.

"You don't know Jack? You'll need to be knowing him if you plan to get by at Tranquila."

"Why's that?"

"You'll see." The driver shrugged and turned his reggae music up, bursting out of the parking lot at a speed that had Paige's pulse rocketing. Looking around for a seatbelt and seeing none, she clutched her purse on her lap and prayed, for the second time that day, that her death wouldn't be imminent. Since conversation seemed to be out, Paige gazed out the window and did her best to take in her new home.

The road they zipped along hugged the water until they got closer to town, where the brightly colored buildings clamored over each other for precious waterfront space. Shops painted in bright gold, brilliant blue, and hot pink were tucked next to restaurants and hotels, and for a small island there seemed to be a fairly vibrant downtown. All five blocks of it, Paige realized, as they cruised through the main drag and back to the winding road in a matter of seconds. That might take some adjustment, she realized, as she saw not a single sign for a Starbucks or a Jamba Juice anywhere to be found. Hotels lined the water on this side of the little town, and Paige eagerly read each sign as they passed, wondering which one was Tranquila Inn. Only when the hotels faded away, as did any other buildings, did Paige begin to wonder if the taxi driver was taking her for a ride.

"Sir? Is it not in that row of hotels?" Paige pitched her voice above the music, and the driver turned and just shook his head at her before continuing to drum the beat of the throbbing music on his steering wheel. Ten minutes later, as they wound along the island, the taxi driver took a sudden left and bumped the taxi down a road overgrown with bushes that slapped against the sides of the van. Paige's eyebrows rose as her stomach did a weird little flip. Was this where he was taking her to kill her? Only when they turned a blind corner and rolled to a stop in front of a large thatched reception hall with a hand-carved sign proclaiming "Tranquila Inn" did Paige let out the breath she'd been holding.

"Let me see the money." The taxi driver turned and looked at her.

"Oh, right." Paige dug in her purse and pulled out a twenty, as well as a few bills for a tip, and a smile spread on the man's face.

"A tip? That's not common here. I like Americans."

"Oh, well, thank you." Paige made a mental note to learn the customs, though she doubted she'd get out of the habit of tipping anytime soon.

Without another word, the driver deposited her bag in front of the taxi, all but hauled Paige out, and tore away before she could rethink her decision. She took a moment to breathe, trying to let her chakras open or whatever Horatio seemed to think she needed, and surveyed her most recent life decision.

Tranquila Inn was comprised of a cluster of thatched cottages that spread out toward the sea, with the main reception area smack dab in the middle. With a high roof, an open-air design, and a scattering of wicker chairs with tropical patterned cushions, the reception hall was breezy and welcoming. Tranquila Inn seemed to live up to its name. Surrounded by green on three sides – the bush that the taxi driver had torn his way through – and the blue of the ocean out front, Paige could now understand why it was set further away from town. It was meant to be an oasis of sorts, she surmised, and picking up her bag, went to find the reception desk.

"Who are you?" A voice like a whiskey-soaked razor blade rasped at her from a cove of bushes by the entrance. Paige shrieked and dropped her bag, holding her hand to her heart as a man, who had previously been crouching, stood to study her.

"Oh my," Paige breathed, looking him up and down.

He was easily over six feet, wearing a baseball hat, sunglasses, and no shirt. Paige had to gulp at the tanned muscles that rippled across his chest. For a moment, her brain slid sideways into a decidedly naughty image of a very sweaty and very sexy island romance, before she caught his scent on the wind from the ocean. Deodorant was obviously not something he believed in. Or cleanliness, for that matter, judging from the dirt and sweat that streaked across those lamentably stunning pecs. Sighing, Paige pushed her fantasies aside and smiled at him.

"Hi, I'm Paige Lowry. I'm looking for reception?"

"We're not open yet."

"Um, aren't you a hotel? As in you're always open?"

"Not until the first group of the season arrives." The man turned as though to leave her, and Paige surprised herself by reaching out to grab his arm — a very muscular arm which Paige barely resisted squeezing. She dropped her hand.

"Wait. I'm not a guest. I work here. Can you direct me to the owner?" Paige assumed he must be a maintenance worker or the gardener, judging from his appearance.

"You work here." It was said in the same tone as someone who'd just found a hair in their food.

"I...I do, yes," Paige said, straightening as he took a long slow look. At five feet three and a quarter inches tall, Paige could credit yoga for keeping her muscular, but there wasn't much she could do about her ample hips or generous bosom. Sometimes her curves got in the way during yoga, not like the much bendier Lily or Nadia—the two women she'd found in her bed not forty-eight hours ago. Sweat dripped down her back, her front – hell, even beneath her boobs – but she held the gardener's eyes – well...his sunglasses – until he looked away.

And cursed.

"And what is it you'll be doing here?" the gardener asked, pulling gloves from his hands and slapping them once before depositing them into the back pocket of his shorts.

"I...well, CeCe hired me to be the new coordinator. She said you'd recently lost one?"

"We didn't lose her. She knew how to find her way out."

"What does that mean?"

"It means she wasn't lost. We told her to go. And it wasn't much of a loss considering she damn well couldn't even manage a spreadsheet."

"Oh. Um." Paige wasn't sure what to say to that. All she knew was that she wanted a shower and a change of clothes, like, yesterday.

"When did you speak with CeCe?" the man said, sighing.

"I'm sorry... who are you?" Paige finally said, trying to gain the upper hand on the conversation.

"The name's Jack. And you?"

"I'm Paige. I just told you that. Is my name that forgettable?" She clamped her lips together when she realized she'd said that last part out loud. A hint of a smile ghosted across Jack's face, and he shook his head once.

"Not at all. Okay, Paige. Welcome to our particular brand of crazy. Let's get you settled."

"What does that mean? Are you the Jack the folks at the airport said to find?"

"That's me, much to my annoyance," Jack said, hefting her duffle bag like it weighed nothing. He strode through the empty reception area, following a gravel path that wound its way to a collection of smaller thatched huts.

"Wait, where are we going? Where's CeCe?"

"I'm taking you to your room. I assume you'll be wanting to change since you're sweating harder than a whore in church, and then I'll be taking you to Ms. CeCe."

"Oh because you're fresh as a daisy?" Whoops, Paige thought as Jack paused and leveled a look at her. Paige pasted a bright smile on her face and he swore softly under his breath and shook his head.

So much for making a good first impression, Paige thought. But she wasn't wrong. It wasn't like this man was all well-appointed himself.

"Let's go."

"Thanks, I guess?" Paige said, not sure she was particularly welcome, and made a note that Jack should definitely not greet any of the incoming guests if this was his attitude.

"Here you are. Key's in the door. There's a safe in the closet for valuables and your passport. Please try to only run the air conditioning at night. Not like it even works most of the time. There's no hot water."

"No hot water?" Paige stopped at the door to the little hut. Painted a bright white, with a palm thatched roof and bright blue shutters on the windows, it seemed simple, happy, and like it would catch the ocean breezes…if she ever opened her windows to this heat.

"You need hot water in this humidity?" Jack gestured with one hand.

"No, I suppose not."

"I'll wait."

"But…I wanted to take a shower."

"Take a shower after. I don't have time to babysit you right now."

"Gee, thanks," Paige bit out and moved into the hut. It had one small room, with a tiny bathroom attached. There was a double bed, a dresser, a small television, a fan, and an air-con unit on the wall. The room was sparse, with little in the way of frills, but frankly, Paige was simply happy to have her own space. Dumping her duffle on the bed, she dug out an airy dress in crimson and changed quickly, cringing at the dampness of her bra. Opting to change that as well, Paige ran a stick of deodorant under her arms and adjusted her hair. Grabbing the key, she locked the door behind her and met Jack where he lounged against a palm tree.

"Pull the shades next time."

"Excuse me?" Paige said, heat lashing her cheeks. "Did you just watch me change?"

"I looked away. Others might not."

"What others? You said you were closed."

"Fine, keep 'em open. I enjoy a peep show on occasion." Jack shrugged and turned, Paige stumbling after him to keep up on the path that curved between the palm trees and around the back side of the reception hall.

"Is there a reason you're being rude to me?" Paige asked, feeling bold.

"You're about to find out," Jack murmured.

"Great, lovely, so happy to be here. You know, as your

new coordinator, I hope this isn't how you greet all your guests."

Jack said nothing as they turned to what looked to be a bar and hangout area. Little tables clustered around a curved bamboo bar where a luscious knockout of a bartender stared daggers, and a couple, dressed for yachting, turned to look at them.

"Well, Jack, who's this? Do you have a new friend?"

The woman was likely to be in her late forties, but it was hard to tell as she may have had some discreet work done. She gave Paige the once-over. This must be CeCe, Paige thought. Dressed in fitted white skinny jeans, a wrap-style fuchsia silk blouse, with a chunky gold braided necklace at her throat, CeCe looked rich, crisply beautiful, and three sheets to the wind. She stumbled a little as she stood from her chair, and the man next to her, handsome in a private school sort of way, grabbed CeCe's arm to steady her.

"I'm Paige Lowry," Paige said, smiling at her.

"That's nice, darling. CeCe Alderidge. And this handsome chap of a man is Whitaker Alderidge, though we call him Whit. Won't you join us for happy hour?"

"I...I'm not sure?" Paige looked from Jack, who said nothing, back to CeCe.

"Don't you drink, darling? Why, everyone has to drink on an island. You can't have happy hour sunsets with none of the happy, no?"

"I'm Paige. Your new employee. You hired me to be your new coordinator?" Paige supplied before CeCe could commandeer a drink for her. She wasn't sure that drinking on her new job would go over all that well. Silence fell on the group as they all turned to look at CeCe and then back to Paige. Confusion crossed CeCe's face, before a wide smile broke out.

"Did I now? Fancy that!" CeCe threw her head back and rocked with laughter, almost falling over before steadying herself on the bar. "Well, in that case, you're definitely entitled to a drink."

Goddess help her, she needed one, Paige decided as she watched Jack slink away, shaking his head. Just what had she gotten herself into?

CHAPTER FOUR

"Paige, darling, an absolute delight to meet you." Whit took her hand and drew her close, his eyes drinking her in, making her feel like she was the only woman in the world. When his gaze dropped momentarily to her cleavage, Paige darted a glance to where CeCe chattered to the bartender. Whit had the look of a man with money who tried to look casually eccentric…his hair just a smidge too long for country club life, and his linen shorts lightly wrinkled. With a martini in one hand, he easily looked like he could be talking about stocks at a stiffly pretentious party as he was propping up the bar at Tranquila Inn. "Aren't you stunning? The local lads will eat you right up."

Paige wasn't entirely sure how to respond to that, but was saved from answering when the bartender interrupted their conversation.

"What will you have?"

"Hi, I'm Paige. I love your necklace. Is it handmade?" Paige asked the beautiful bartender. She'd worked in customer service for years, and she knew it was always important to be respectful of the person serving her. Though the woman had looked murderous when she'd first arrived in tow behind Jack, now her expression softened slightly at Paige's words.

"My daughter made it for me. I'm Mariposa, by the way," she said. Her necklace was a simple white cowrie shell strung on a leather cord with two turquoise beads on either side. It might not have been fancy like CeCe's chunky gold necklace, but against Mariposa's tanned skin and wild dark curls, it looked exotic.

"Nice to meet you, Mariposa. How old is your daughter?"

"She's eleven going on thirty," Mariposa finally smiled, causing Paige to catch her breath. This woman could easily be on the front cover of magazines.

"Weren't we all at that age?" CeCe trilled, waving her hand in the air. "I thought I knew everything about the world and nobody could tell me differently."

"Not much has changed, love, has it?" Whit said, wrapping an arm around CeCe's waist.

"I suppose not, darling." CeCe tossed her blond hair and laughed a robust laugh. It was the type of laugh meant to draw attention to her – the scratch of a record during a party – and Paige suspected she knew exactly what she was about. This was a woman who did not enjoy sharing the limelight. How she had hired a woman like Mariposa was beyond Paige, since despite CeCe's loud personality, all eyes would go to the bartender.

"I'll have something light…" Paige turned to Mariposa, "A prosecco maybe? Or a light wine?"

"Will a rosé do you?" Mariposa asked.

"Yes, that will be perfect. Thanks." Paige had quickly surmised that a drink was exactly the thing she would need to get through this introduction.

"Sit, sit, please," Whit said, pulling out a bamboo stool next to the bar.

"I'll just tell chef we have one more for dinner," CeCe said, floating away with her martini in hand and calling for the chef. Paige wondered if there would be name cards at dinner, or if they were just doing their best to put on fancy airs when this hotel clearly didn't call for it. Accepting her drink with a grateful smile, Paige took a small sip and turned to study the lounge area. While the hotel wasn't fancy, it wasn't run-down or in disrepair either. If anything, it struck the right notes between offbeat charming and relaxing oasis. Under the large thatched roof of the open-air reception hall, wicker chairs and low-slung couches were clustered together in various conversation and eating areas. A tropical banana leaf print covered the chair cushions, and far above their heads, huge bamboo fans and wicker basket-style lanterns hung from the roof. The soft pulse of reggae music encouraged the island vibe, and Paige found her foot tapping to the beat. The building itself was positioned well to catch the breezes from the ocean, and Paige could imagine it would be easy to relax here over drinks while looking out to the water for dolphins.

"Do you get dolphins here?" Paige asked, turning to Whit.

"Of course the dolphins visit us," Whit said as though it was the most natural occurrence in the world. "As do eels, stingrays, and if we're lucky enough, a few pilot whales."

"The dolphins come by late afternoon. They have a routine. You can go out and swim with them," Mariposa supplied as she took a sip of her Sprite. Paige wondered if she didn't drink or just didn't drink on the job. It was hard to get a read on her employers so far, and Jack had high-tailed it as soon as he'd dumped her at the bar.

"That's pretty amazing." Paige smiled. "I'm sure your guests love that." So would she, Paige thought, and made a mental note to slip away one day and get in the water with the dolphins.

"They do, they really do," Whit said, leaning one arm on the bar and smiling down at her. "Tell me, gorgeous, what is it you did in the States again?"

"Um," Paige blinked at his words, and caught Mariposa rolling her eyes behind his back. "I was a business coordinator for a yoga studio. In fact, for the studio that was meant to come here next week for the upcoming yoga retreat."

"Ah, a business coordinator. Sounds absolutely smashing. Doesn't it, Mariposa?"

"Does it?" Mariposa questioned Whit who completely ignored her dark look.

"I do admire a woman with brains. I'm sure it took you positively ages to deal with all the ins and outs of running such a business. You'll have to tell me all about it one night."

Before Paige could issue a gentle reprimand of her employer's blatant advances, CeCe floated back into the room, her martini glass empty and her eyes bright.

"The chef will be delighted to add you to the menu. He has some lovely pieces of fresh-caught tuna tonight. Have I told you about the time I was in Sardinia? The seafood there…" CeCe sighed and brought her hands to her lips and made a kissing noise.

"Um, no, I haven't heard…" Paige said, taking another sip from her drink.

"Oh, darling, you must go. It's simply to die for. But you know, not much time for travel these days. I'm just so busy all the time. We have so many projects, you know," CeCe said, brushing a wayward lock of blond hair back from her cheek and accepting a fresh martini from Mariposa.

"Right," Paige nodded, glancing around at the empty hotel. "I'm sure there's much to do to run a place like this."

"Soooo much," CeCe drawled. She climbed onto a stool and crossed her legs neatly, smoothing her pants and smiling brightly at Paige. "You must tell me everything about yourself, gorgeous. I'm sure you've an enlightening story to share."

Hmm, Paige thought, were both her employers hitting on her? Perhaps they were swingers? Or maybe it was just the way they talked? Deciding to reserve judgement for now, otherwise she'd run screaming back to the airport, Paige took a deep breath and recapped the story she'd already told to CeCe over the phone.

"Dearest Paige, what a tragic thing to have happen to you," Whit said with mournful eyes. Reaching out, he squeezed her hand. "I can only hope your time at Tranquila Inn will allow for you to release the past."

"I'm not sure that tragic is the word for it. Expected, maybe"— CeCe tapped a finger against her lips —"As men tend to wander. Nevertheless, I don't think I like the sound of this Horatio. He seems to be quite the cad, and I'm certain you're the better for being here. We are in desperate need of your help. We're just so busy, you know."

Again, Paige couldn't help but glance to the empty reception area and then back to Mariposa. This time, the bartender just pressed her lips together and gave a little shrug of her shoulders. Perhaps CeCe's obsession with being so busy kept her occupied enough not to realize they weren't *actually* busy?

"Sure, well, I'm happy to help ease that burden a bit. I'd love to get started. Are there any books I can look at? Calendars? Schedules? Oh, and I'll need to sign an employment contract, of course," Paige trailed off as both Whit and CeCe stared at her like she'd thrown a cockroach in their face.

"They don't like to talk about work during happy hour. One does not mix the two," Mariposa supplied.

"But…it's not even happy hour…" Paige stopped as the look of disgust deepened on both her employers' faces. "I meant to say…sure, of course, we should relax and get to know each other first."

"That's right, darling. You've just traveled all this way from…" CeCe arched a brow at her.

"California." Paige sighed and took a large gulp of her wine.

"Of course. What a long way to come! There's plenty of time for work talk tomorrow. You need to relax, have a drink, enjoy yourself. Take it poco poco, as the locals say."

"I guess we do have time since the retreat's been cancelled," Paige mused, knowing that Yoga Soulone's retreat had been meant to fill up the entire hotel for the next three weeks. "Is that what poco poco means then? Take it slow?"

"Yes, slow or easy. Much like Tranquila," Mariposa said, reaching across the bar to top off Paige's glass, though she hadn't requested it. "Why rush? So you can race your way to death?"

"Um," Paige said, not sure how to respond to that.

"She's absolutely right, you know," Whit smiled over at her, his teeth blindingly white in his tanned face. "Life is meant to be savored slowly, like you're eating at a buffet. Why load your first plate up with everything and then exhaust yourself? It's best to take a small salad plate and sample as you go. You'll enjoy more and your energy is preserved."

"Right," Paige said, and wondered if that was also his attitude when it came to other women. She was completely unsure how to proceed with these two. "You're talking about mindfulness. Living life in a mindful manner causes you to slow down and appreciate the little moments."

"That's exactly it. Aren't you just exquisite?" Whit applauded her like she was the prize dog who'd just won best in show. "Now, tell me, what have you been reading lately? I've just done a deep dive into Scientology, and I find it fascinating how they've roped people into believing their ways."

"Oh, don't go on and bore us with your latest books,

darling. Don't you see the girl is knackered? She's been traveling. She needs more wine and less interrogation."

"It's hardly…" Paige looked between the two. "I don't…"

"I'm certainly not interrogating the girl by asking what she's been reading," Whit said.

"Of course not, darling. But you don't really care about her books. You just wanted to use it as a jumping-off point to talk about what you've been reading," CeCe said, smiling though her voice sliced like razors. At least it sounded that way to Paige, though Whit didn't even flinch.

"Categorically untrue. Perhaps she's reading the same book? Or has read it? Then we'd have a mutual topic to discuss. It's as though you've forgotten how to have good dinner conversation, darling." Whit smiled at his wife and for all Paige could read, he was not remotely bothered by the ice in CeCe's voice.

"We're not at dinner, are we? And, I do admit, this island does strain dreadfully on my manners at times. We do the best we can, don't we, darling?"

"We certainly do, my love."

Paige couldn't decide if they were intensely drunk, intensely crazy, or a perfect combination of both.

"You'll get used to them," Mariposa said, leaning on the bar near Paige as the couple began to chatter at each other. "They're…a lot to take in."

"I guess I'm trying to decide if I actually have a job here or not. CeCe seems to have no recollection of hiring me."

"There's no surprise there. Don't worry. Jack will sort it out."

"Is he…I thought he was the gardener?" Paige asked.

"Jack's the backbone. Luis is the gardener. Be nice to him or I'll cut you." Mariposa turned away. Paige's eyebrows rose. Surely, the woman had meant she'd cut her off…as in cut her off from alcohol. Swallowing, Paige turned back when CeCe tapped her leg.

"Tell me, dear, do you know how to do acrobatics? Absolutely fascinating body work, really. I'm sure it's just like yoga…"

Paige drained her glass.

CHAPTER FIVE

Dinner was…a production. A tragic one at that.

Paige watched, wide-eyed, as CeCe fluttered about, rearranging plates, and insisting people move until she had everything exactly the way she wanted it.

"I like pairing people who don't usually sit together next to each other," CeCe explained. "It encourages different conversations."

Paige examined the table and pressed her lips together. As she was the only new person at the table, she could only wonder if this was a nightly event or if CeCe was putting this on for her benefit. Jack sat, stone-faced, at one corner of the table, steadfastly refusing to move even when CeCe shot him an annoyed look. He'd cleaned up since Paige had last spoken with him and wore a simple white t-shirt and khaki shorts. His feet were bare, something CeCe had commented on, and Jack had also ignored. Paige wondered what his relationship with his employers was, as it was clear he had some sort of upper hand over them.

He'd yet to speak to her again, and now she was even more curious about his story.

"This is Luis, our gardener, and Martin, our chef."

CeCe pulled her attention back to where two men stood at the end of the table. Martin was a towering man with brown skin and an apron tied at his waist; and the other, Luis, was handsome in a pretty way – as though he paid great attention to his skin and hair care. Paige quickly understood why Mariposa had warned her about being mean to Luis. Paige wondered what the attitude about homosexuality was on the island.

"Nice to meet you both. I'm Paige, and I'm the new events coordinator here." Paige stood and shook both of their hands.

"A new coordinator? Oh, that's fantastic. I have some ideas about introducing herbal teas or even gardening as meditation practice for the retreats. Would that be something of interest to you?" Luis asked, smiling at her with perfect white teeth.

"Absolutely," Paige assured him. "Once I can get an understanding of how things are run, I'm certain I can incorporate ideas like that for guests. I'd love to hear more about what you have to offer."

"Hmm, already better than the last coordinator," Luis said. "She was too full of herself to even listen to any of my ideas."

"She was just very busy, darling. We all are, you know," CeCe chided Luis and pointed at a chair for him to sit in.

"More like she was busy stealing money," Luis muttered, but Paige caught it and raised her eyebrows at him. He shook his head slightly to discourage her from asking anything further.

"Paige, darling, come sit by Jack. It would do him well to have actual dinner conversation for once."

"That's really not necessary," Jack sighed. "I just want to eat my food and get back to work."

"It's night. What's there to work on, dearest boy?" Whit laughed and raised a glass to him. "It's time to relax."

"I need to go over the accounts and figure out how we're going to afford your new hire," Jack said, his words like a splash of cold water on the table. Luis sniffed and looked away, while the chef turned on his heel and disappeared into the back room. Paige's stomach turned at his words and she looked to where CeCe stood, her face sad as she shook her head at Jack.

"Jack, you're well aware that CeCe doesn't like to talk work at dinner," Whit chided.

"Or ever, really," Jack muttered.

"Dinner is served!" Martin boomed as he returned, wheeling a cart in front of him.

"Is Mariposa joining us?" Paige asked, trying to change the subject as she eased into the chair next to Jack. They sat at a long table on the other side of the reception hall, beneath two palm leaf fans that gently moved the air around them. Though the fans helped with air movement, the humidity still pressed on Paige's skin like a wet blanket. She'd applied a natural bug repellent as the sun had gone down and the mosquitos had appeared out of nowhere. The others had promised that she would get used to them, but Paige wasn't so sure.

"She had to go pick up her daughter. It will be self-service at the bar tonight if you want more to drink," Jack said.

"What happens when guests are here? Is it self-service then? Like an honor system?"

"She'll stay late when guests are here. We've had a few guests stretch the honor system when we tried that."

"Ah, that's unfortunate," Paige said, and smiled up at Martin as he placed a dish in front of her. "This looks lovely, thank you."

"A simple meal, but with big taste," Martin promised her.

"Those are the best kind," Paige agreed and he beamed at her before moving on. Paige's eyebrow rose when he plated and then sat at the end of the table, but she supposed this was kind of like a family dinner of sorts. Her food did look delicious – tuna, mixed vegetables, and seasoned rice. Her stomach grumbled, as she hadn't eaten since breakfast. The wine had made her feel loose, and she was starting to enjoy the ridiculousness that was CeCe and Whit.

"Darlings! Let's all welcome Paige to the Tranquila Inn family," CeCe raised her glass at the head of the table and everyone else, except for Jack, did the same. "May Poco Poco Island work its magic on you as it has on all of us. Cheers to sunny days and languid nights."

They all dug into their food, though Paige had to wonder if CeCe had actually meant liquid nights. Looking across the table, she saw that CeCe and Whit were leaned close to each other, hotly debating something about a submarine that had sunk off the coast of England years ago, and Luis and Martin chattered to each other in rapid Spanish. Which left her surly dinner companion, Jack.

"So, how long have you been on the island?"

"I came here to help renovate and clean up Tranquila Inn after the last big storm." Jack stabbed a piece of tuna with his fork.

Shocked, Paige gaped at him.

"Do you get big storms here? Hurricanes?"

"We are in the hurricane belt. What did you think that meant?" Jack looked at her like she'd just told him the sky was red.

"I didn't realize Poco Poco Island was in the hurricane belt. I'm from California. Earthquakes are our jam."

"Could you imagine?" Luis gasped and put his hand to his chest. "Buildings shaking and everything falling from the shelves? It must be horrifying."

"But you're okay with hurricanes?" Paige laughed. "Aren't they quite devastating?"

"Depends on the category." Luis shrugged. "We haven't had a really big one in ages, so I'm sure we're due for one. You just have to be smart and prepare for it. You can't live your life worrying about a potential storm."

A hurricane seemed like the least of her worries at the moment, Paige thought, and bent her head to her food.

CHAPTER SIX

Too keyed up to sleep, Paige found her way to the beach later that night. She'd successfully navigated her way out of after-dinner drinks, and instead had retreated to her cabin to…just lie on the bed and stare at the ceiling. When it was clear that sleep wasn't coming anytime soon, the call of the waves outside had been too much for her to resist. Wrapping a sarong loosely around her body, Paige had padded silently to the beach with only the moon to light her way. Now she sat, huddled on a lounge chair, and contemplated where she'd landed.

This wasn't the first time an impulsive decision had gotten her into sticky situations, but this was certainly the most potentially damaging one. Her bank balance was at an all-time low, and with no safety net, she needed this job to work out for her. At least until she could figure out her next steps. Now, Paige had no idea what – or if – she'd be getting paid, let alone how she could afford to get herself off this island if she needed to.

It looked like she had booked a one-way ticket into learning to accept her life choices.

"I could hear your big sighs all the way across the beach."

Paige jumped at the voice that reached her through the darkness.

"Pity-party of one, please." Paige glared in the direction of the voice, and waited until Jack strolled into view.

"Ah, too bad, I do enjoy a good sulk," Jack said, dropping to the lounger next to her. "I prefer mine with a glass of good whiskey and a cigar, but I suppose a moody ocean under the moonlight will do the trick."

Amused despite herself, Paige shot him a look.

"I'm not sulking."

"That pouty lower lip says differently, but I'll play along. If you're not sulking, then what are you doing?" Jack leaned back in the chair and crossed his arms over his head. His shirt looked bright white in the moonlight, as did the smile he flashed at her.

"I'm contemplating," Paige clarified.

"Ah, a dangerous pastime, if I do say so myself."

"Not one for deep moments of reflection, are you?" Paige slanted a look at him before turning back to where the light of the moon trailed a gentle path across the water.

"While I do my best to avoid them, even I have my moments, I suppose."

"Well, welcome to mine."

"And what are we reflecting on this evening?"

"Safety," Paige surprised herself by saying.

"It's pretty safe here. Though I wouldn't advise you wander onto a beach near town late at night alone."

"Oh, I mean more like in, you know, life choices. Financial decisions. Jumping without looking first. That kind of thinking. I'm feeling like I forgot to put on my parachute."

"Ah," Jack said.

Paige waited a moment and then huffed out a little breath when no more was forthcoming.

"A man of few words, are you?"

"Well, you didn't ask me for advice, and you didn't elaborate on your problems, so there wasn't much for me to offer now, was there?"

The man had a point, Paige realized, and stretched her legs out in front of her. The tension that knotted her stomach began to ease as the rhythm of the ocean soothed her.

"That's actually a nice trait you have there, Jack."

"What's that?"

"Not rushing to tell me what to do or man-splain something to me."

"I fix enough problems around here. It can get tiring. Plus, I've just met you. I can't presume to have any answers for you that you haven't already considered."

"Well, you might, actually." Paige turned to look at him again. Inexplicably, she wanted to reach out a hand to touch him...or run a finger over the smooth muscles that rippled in his arms. Bad girl, Paige warned herself. No sleeping with the boss. If he was even her boss. It was yet to be determined.

"What can I do for you?"

"Well, that finances thing I mentioned? I find myself in a precarious position of desperately needing them."

"Like how desperate? You running from a gambling problem or something?" The moon glinted off Jack's eyes as he turned to her.

"No! Oh my god. No. Nothing like that. Just…well, I made shit for money working at Yoga Soulone. Horatio did almost everything on a trade and I just fell into the life-style. It didn't give me much room to save. I don't spend a lot. But I also don't have a lot. Do you really think CeCe won't be able to pay me?"

"You'll get paid. I'll take care of it." The words were like a cooling balm to the anxiety that clawed through her every time she thought about money.

"I would greatly appreciate that. Um…"

"Yes?"

"How much? To be precise?" Paige's voice went up a notch as she asked.

"I'll have to doublecheck the contracts tomorrow." Then Jack quoted her a price that made her close her eyes and whisper a silent "thank-you" to the universe.

"That would be most welcome. Thank you."

"Now that we've sorted that out, are you done contemplating for the night?"

"I don't know." Paige laughed again, relaxing back against the chair. "I do think I have a lot to process."

"What's there to process? You move to a new country. Start a new job. Meet new people. Have fun. Rinse and repeat."

"Is it so easy for you then?" Paige tilted her head to study him. What an interesting life he must lead, she thought, where he didn't blink twice at moving to another country.

"Yes, it can be. But let me tell you something about island life...don't get too attached to people."

"Why's that?"

"Well, I should amend that. Don't get too attached to people like you."

"What's that supposed to mean?" Paige glared at Jack and was rewarded with that flash of grin again that sent a low tug of heat through her stomach.

"You're transient is all."

"Did you just call me a transient?" Paige pulled her head back like he'd just called her a grave robber. "That makes me sound like I'm homeless or something."

"I mean, you kind of are, right? Without this job... where would you stay? Do you have a house in the States?"

"Nope, the Ex got custody of that." Paige picked at the fringes on her sarong.

"See?" Jack laughed before she could respond. "But what I meant is that people breeze through to work on an island and they leave. Particularly in the hospitality industry. You get used to people taking a cool summer job or interning, but they don't stay. It's a transient kind of lifestyle. It makes it difficult for people who are here long-term to get attached, is all."

"Ah, gotcha. Be careful not to fall for me, then," Paige quipped and then pressed her lips together. *Eeeek!* Why did she just say that? When she was rewarded with another laugh, Paige let out the breath she'd been holding.

"I'll try my hardest. But I'll warn you – I'm hard to resist."

"Oh, is that a challenge?" Paige turned and lifted an eyebrow at him. He was grinning at her in the darkness.

"Not much of a challenge, is it, sweets? I saw how you looked at me when you arrived."

"Oh…you're an ass!" Paige couldn't help but laugh at him though, as his grin widened on his face. "And that look was my disgust at your smell."

"Ah, you'll get used to it. We all sweat here." Jack shrugged it off.

"Or was it at your rudeness?" Paige tapped a finger to her lips as she thought about it.

"Treat 'em mean…keep 'em keen."

This time Jack full on belly-laughed when she whirled on him.

"Oh, you're going to be fun to poke. Don't stay out here too long or you'll fall asleep and get eaten alive by the sand flies in the morning." Jack stood up.

"Well, that sounds just lovely." Paige looked up at where Jack had stopped at the end of the chair. "You don't have to worry about me, I can take care of myself."

"Says the woman out here contemplating how she ended up in an uncertain job position with no way off the island." Jack gentled his words with a soft smile. "For what it's worth – I think it's pretty great of you to have taken the leap. Fortune favors the brave and all…" With that, Jack sauntered into the darkness leaving a warm glow coursing through her. Moments before, she'd been certain she'd just made the worst decision of her life.

Now, Paige realized that Jack was right. She *was* brave. And there was nothing standing in the way of her making this island-life a reality.

CHAPTER SEVEN

Surprisingly, Paige slept soundly for the first time in days. Perhaps it was the lack of sleep catching up with her or the several glasses of wine she'd had, but once she'd returned to her little cabin, it had taken all of Paige's willpower to force herself to have a quick shower before crawling naked into bed. Now, as the first light of morning slipped through her windows, Paige stretched and stared up at the ceiling where a fan wafted cool puffs of air over her skin. Sometime during the night, she had kicked off her sheet, and now she lay naked across the double bed. Paige took a moment, as she did every morning, to take a few deep breaths and to center herself. While Horatio may have been on the extreme end of the mindfulness culture, she still felt there were actual benefits to a daily practice of yoga and meditation.

Once she'd centered herself, Paige allowed her mind to drift over her impressions from the night before. There was no doubt that CeCe and Whit would be a handful. She'd have to carefully monitor their behavior around the guests. But with a few more weeks to get settled before the next retreat would arrive, Paige was sure she could learn the best way to manage her new employers.

Somewhere, a wind chime tingled charmingly in the ocean breeze, and Paige finally worked up the energy to pull herself from bed. Standing, she did a series of full body stretches at the end of the bed and then gasped when she looked out the window. Jack stood, a shit-eating grin on his face, holding a coconut in one hand and a machete in the other. Paige squealed and dove out of the way of the window.

He'd warned her about pulling the shades, hadn't he? Paige slapped a hand to her face and duck-walked across the cabin to dig in her bag until she found her bikini. Pulling it on while she muttered a long string of decidedly not-mindful curses, Paige finally stood and wrapped a sarong around her waist. Flinging the door to her cottage open, Paige glowered at Jack.

"I'm not your peep show, you know."

"I was just coming to offer you a coconut for some fresh juice this morning." Jack shrugged. "I believe I mentioned pulling the shades yesterday?"

"You did. But I didn't expect anyone to be creeping around this early."

The grin on Jack's face widened. It didn't help that he was back to just wearing a low-slung pair of board shorts, and his tanned chest rippled with muscles. It was hard to be mad at him when her mind immediately slipped to other more interesting pursuits.

"It's hardly creeping when there are dozens of other

cottages around you. You'll learn most island people are up early as it helps to get things done before the heat of the day settles in."

"Is that why people siesta in the afternoon?" Paige asked.

"Yes, you'll find most places close for a longer lunch here as well. Typically an hour and a half to two hours."

"Were you really bringing me a coconut?" Paige leaned against the door frame and narrowed her eyes at him.

"I was. Maybe I can charm you into staying around longer than the last coordinator."

"The one who stole from you?" Paige crossed her arms over her chest and leaned against her doorway.

"Ah, yes. That one."

"I thought you kicked her out." Paige wandered closer to him and tilted her head to look up at his face. His eyes weren't shaded by sunglasses today and the bright blue popped in his tanned face. "Which I do not blame you for at all, by the way. I just hope you don't hold me accountable for her past mistakes."

Jack grimaced and crouched at her feet, motioning for her to step back as he swung the machete down onto the coconut's shell.

"I have no problem letting someone prove themselves. But CeCe's track record in hiring people is less than stellar." Thwack! Another cut into the hull.

"Is that so?"

"It is." Thwack! "And I'm the one who ends up cleaning up the messes."

"I'm sorry. That has to be annoying."

"Frustrating." Thwack! A splinter of the hull went flying and Paige stepped back uneasily. "But I'm used to it by now. It just sometimes takes me a minute to recalibrate."

"So… you think I'm a bad decision," Paige said.

Jack stood and turned, handing her the coconut that had now been cut open so she could drink from the core.

"Drink and I'll cut the meat out once you are finished."

"Thank you." Paige accepted the coconut and brought it to her lips, enjoying the simple flavor of fresh coconut water. She'd always bought the little packaged cartons of coconut water sold at the yoga studio, but it was much better straight from the source.

"I don't know that you're a bad decision as of yet," Jack said, standing and tossing the machete back and forth lightly in his hands. Paige wondered if he had any idea how intimidating he looked. "We will need a point person for the retreats, and I've been told my customer service skills are lacking."

"Shocking," Paige murmured and was rewarded with a laugh.

"I *can* be good with the guests. I just prefer to interact with them in small doses. Plus, there's always a million things to get done around here so my time is limited."

"What exactly is it you do?" Paige asked and then drained the coconut of its juice. Handing it back to him, she watched as he crouched and brought the machete up into the air again.

"A little bit of everything. I guess you could say I'm the manager. I look over the accounts, help with orders, meet with the cleaning staff, maintenance…that kind of thing."

"You're a one-man show, it sounds like."

"I have to be. That's one thing you'll learn about island life – that you have to be adaptable."

"I can adapt." Paige did a little curtsy in her sarong. "I am here to serve, good sir."

"Thank god. We need the help. As you can see, it's a bit of a skeleton staff and retreats can be…demanding."

"Trust me, I know. Try running retreats for rich Californians who'd rather take influencer photos than meditate and be quiet. Why in the world would you sign up for a silent meditation retreat if you were just going to sneak out and smoke weed and chatter on your phone all day?"

"Ah…" Jack shook his head. "I can't answer that question. It sounds like people who have disposable income and don't follow directions well."

"I've gotten used to managing all personalities." Paige put on her customer service smile and affected a cheerful but soothing tone. "So nice of you to join us today, Mrs. Phillips. I must say, that shade of coral really does flattering things for your skin tone. Would you like me to take a photo of you? Perhaps over by the palm? The lighting is just fantastic at this time of the morning. After that, might I suggest a meditative swim in the ocean? There's nothing like connecting with nature to really open the flow of energy to your chakras."

Jack threw back his head and laughed, and Paige grinned.

"Okay, I'm feeling much more confident in having you

on board. That's just the amount of handholding we want here."

"I'm used to dealing with everything from fragile egos to earth mamas to influencer models. It's all part of the package when you are working in the health and wellness world."

"It sounds complicated. Why did you get involved if you don't believe in it?"

"Oh, I do believe in it." Paige looked at him in surprise. "I think the basic core tenets of the wellness world are incredibly beneficial. But for me that boils down to move your body more and try to meditate or at the very least be mindful in your approach to things."

"I can get behind that. Move your body more and spend time not talking."

Paige laughed and took a bite of the chewy coconut as she leaned back against a palm tree.

"Is that your way of describing meditating? Spending time not talking?"

"It's one and the same, right?"

"I mean…in theory, yes. But there's a bit more to the practice."

"Maybe you can teach me someday. I guess I find my own meditation in some of the repetitive work I do around here. Helping Luis in the gardens or going for a swim, that kind of thing."

"I'm sure anything that lets your mind rest for a moment can be considered meditation. I believe it's a personal thing – so I'm not one to scold you for not properly meditating."

"Thank goodness. There's nothing like a good scolding

to bring out the bad boy in me." Jack grinned at her and Paige felt a little heat wash over her. She really needed to get control of her hormones if she was going to be around Jack while he had no shirt on. It wasn't like she wasn't used to seeing muscular men where she came from. It was just that there was something so decidedly masculine about Jack. He was just someone who looked like he could handle anything that came his way and that would extend to the bedroom as well.

"Rest assured, I won't be walking around here with a whip."

"More's the pity," Jack mumbled and handed her more coconut before she could reply. Scrambling for something else to say, Paige chewed for a moment to buy time.

"And despite my disheveled appearance yesterday, I am actually quite organized. In fact, if you can lead me to coffee, I'd love to dive right into the books and get an idea of the upcoming season," Paige said.

"I have no problem doing that. It's best you get started." Jack motioned her to follow and Paige looked down at her sarong.

"Wait, don't I need to change?"

"No bother. It's just our little crew at the hotel today. Plus, island life is much more casual. I suspect you'll want to get a handle on things as the next retreat starts in three days."

"Wait...what?" Paige raced forward and grabbed Jack's arms to stall him in his tracks. "I thought Yoga Soulone was the next retreat. I cancelled that retreat *specifically* when I called CeCe."

"I don't know the studio name, but I can tell you the

retreat has not been cancelled. From my understanding, they arrive in three days."

A piece of coconut dropped from Paige's hands as dread filled her.

Horatio was coming to Poco Poco Island.

CHAPTER EIGHT

"How can this be?" Paige muttered, shuffling through papers on the desk. She had barely blinked at the chaos that greeted her when Jack had let her into the office. Disorder had been the norm for Horatio as he preferred to let someone else clean up the messes he made. She'd gotten to the point of wondering if he was even capable of seeing the confusion he created or if he simply didn't care? Either way, her new office felt familiar to her. A large desk had been positioned beneath a window with a view to the reception hall, and a long bookshelf and a set of filing cabinets lined another wall. Paige could only guess at the state of the filing cabinets, but based on the mounds of paper strewn across her desk, she could imagine it wasn't pretty.

"What seems to be the problem? This is a three-week retreat from my understanding. I know it's quick for you to jump in and learn the lay of the land, but we'll all help you," Jack said. He leaned against the door jamb, his muscular arms crossed over his chest, a faint hint of worry in his eyes. "If this throws you already, I'll admit I'm a bit worried about your qualifications."

"Oh, shut it," Paige muttered, digging deeper into the piles of paper. Sure, it was rude of her to speak to a co-worker like that – or perhaps maybe her boss for all she knew – but since the man had just seen her naked, she figured they were past any formalities. "I can run a retreat in my sleep. It's the fact that it's Yoga Soulone."

"And?"

"Were you not there for…" Paige trailed off as she glanced up at him. That's right, he had dumped her at the bar last night and left, so he'd missed out on her story about Horatio. "Ah, that's right. You missed story time last night. Short version – this is the studio that I used to work for and run. I was also involved with the owner. The Ex that I mentioned to you? Unbeknownst to me, his open-door policy included not just his studio hours but also his bedroom."

"Ah. And this is the man who is arriving here in…" Jack glanced at the calendar tacked to the wall that show-cased a bright photo of an angel fish. "Three days time?"

"Correct. Though I cancelled the retreat and CeCe knew that. She hired me when I called to cancel."

"Listen…" Jack edged his way into the office. "CeCe talks. A lot. She's flighty on her best days. Her heart is generally always in a good place, but reliable is not the word to describe our dear CeCe. It's quite likely the studio reinstated the retreat and she didn't think a thing of it."

"That's a terrifying way to run a business," Paige decided.

"It is. Which is why we need a coordinator. Not only to run the retreats, but to run interference with CeCe."

"What does Whit do, exactly?" Paige wondered. From her estimation, he'd seemed fairly on-the-ball if not slightly overzealous when it came to flirtations.

"That's an excellent question, Paige. I'll let you know when I find out." Jack sighed and squeezed the bridge of his nose. "Listen, I'm sorry your cheating scum of an ex-boyfriend is coming down here. But we really need the money and we need good reviews of Tranquila Inn. Yoga Soulone is a studio that has wealthy clientele and we need them to go home and brag to their equally-as-wealthy friends. Is there any chance you can consider ignoring Horatio for the duration and just do a kick-ass job for us?"

Paige plopped down in the seat behind the desk and considered his words.

"I don't like him. I really don't. In fact, over the days since I've left, I've allowed all the things that annoyed me about him to finally rise to the surface. He's a guru-type guy in the worst possible way. He feeds on lonely women and believes his own hype. There isn't a bribe that Horatio has ever turned down – he always says it's rude not to accept gifts. He lures these women, and some men, too, into gifting him all sorts of ridiculous things and sells them on the belief that his classes will heal the darkness inside of them. It's a con – a long con – and one that he does incredibly well. His ego is larger than this hotel and he won't take well to not being in control, let alone exalted. We'd have to basically bow to him and his every whim."

"And? Isn't that what customer service is based on? Making the customer feel like they walk on water?"

"Ugh." Paige felt her stomach twist. It was no use. She could run, she could hide, but one way or another, it looked like she was going to have to face her past head-on. Considering she didn't currently have the funds for another ticket to fly off the island, it looked like Paige was going to have to put her big girl pants on and deal with Horatio.

"What kind of name is Horatio?"

"A self-given one. His real name is Paul, but he'd kill me if I let people know that."

"Why in the world would anyone choose Horatio over Paul? What's wrong with Paul?"

"Horatio had more mystique to it."

"Wasn't Horatio the only one who survived in *Hamlet*?"

Surprised, Paige glanced at Jack. "You read Shakespeare?"

"I mean, didn't we all have to read Hamlet at some point in school?"

"I guess. But yes, Horatio survives after watching everything fall apart. It's certainly appropriate for my… this Horatio. He leaves tragedy in his wake with casual aplomb," Paige said morosely.

"Well, buck up, buttercup. You've got work to do. I was able to pull most of the information together and put it on your desk. I trust you'll remain professional through this retreat."

"I shall do my best," Paige said, flipping through a file.

"How about…yes, Jack, I promise not to let Horatio get the best of me now that I am employed by Tranquila Inn."

"Am I, though? I've yet to sign a contract and I have no idea how I'll be paid."

"Check the red folder. I put it together for you last night."

"Thank you." Paige shot him a smile. "Listen, this… shook me a bit. But I can promise you that I'm a fairly steady person, and I will handle this retreat well for you. Now, if you can just point me in the direction of coffee, I'd be more than delighted to dig in."

"Coffee's through to the kitchen. Chef doesn't mind if you pop in during the mornings. He usually puts out fruit and some sort of food along with coffee and we all come through to graze when we feel like it."

"When should I expect CeCe and Whit?"

"That's anyone's guess. Usually not before mid-day, I'd say."

"But…" Paige's mouth dropped open. "That's half the day gone. The yogis will be up with the sunrise for morning meditation."

"And I'm sure that CeCe and Whit will wish them well with their morning routines. But they, themselves, do not practice an early start to the day."

"So you're saying I'll need to be flexible with my expectations of them?" Paige nodded and stood. She quickly untied the sarong at her waist and wound it around her body to tie at her neck so as to form a makeshift dress. While Paige was comfortable in her body, she still felt better covering herself if she was going to be wandering into the kitchen for food.

"I would highly suggest mastering the art of adapt-ability when it comes to living life on an island…in general." Jack laughed. "Nothing ever proceeds smoothly and any task you hope to accomplish generally takes twice the amount of time. That being said, I've got to get on with my day."

"Yeah, yeah, go solve all the problems then while I sort this desk out."

"Of course, I will. That's why they call me Jack." Jack shot her that killer grin again before sliding out the door. "Jack of all trades."

CHAPTER NINE

Paige all but forgot coffee as she returned to her office after a quick change of clothes and attacked the stack of papers on her desk. When she could no longer resist the siren song of caffeine, she stretched and stood – slipping her feet into the ballet flats under her desk. Paige let out a scream as pain shot up her leg. She dropped to the floor and pulled her shoe off, screaming once more as a yellow insect dropped from her shoe and scuttled across the floor.

A knock sounded sharply at her door.

"Come in," Paige gasped. Tears sprung to her eyes, but she'd frozen in place, unsure of what to do.

Luis poked his head inside.

"You okay, mama? I heard you scream."

"I...that thing...stung..." Paige blinked as her vision blurred.

"Scorpion." Luis turned and whistled sharply. "Get the first aid kit."

"It really hurts. Be careful," Paige said.

"I've got my gardening gloves on. Gotta protect my

manicure." Luis held up his gloved hands and then bent, effortlessly scooping the scorpion between his palms and then disappearing outside. When a shadow fell across the floor, Paige assumed it was Luis returning.

"Thank you for getting rid of it for me."

"I'll tell Luis. He's off to find it a safe spot away from the cabin."

"Oh." Paige blinked up at Jack, as he crouched next to her with a first-aid kit. "Why doesn't he kill it?"

"Because it's not the scorpion's fault. He thought he'd found a safe spot. He was just protecting himself."

"Nasty little shit," Paige grimaced as Jack took her foot in his hand. She wasn't ready to view the little bug in a kind light.

"Yeah, I can't say I enjoy their stings either. Particularly if it happens when you're sleeping."

"When you're...please don't tell me that." Paige held up her hand. "Do not say another word. I will never sleep again if I think too much about it."

"It's pretty rare that they end up there."

"And yet, you're still talking..." Paige glared at Jack.

He laughed, and cradled her foot in his lap. Cool blue eyes met hers.

"How do you feel?"

"Cranky."

"I can imagine. But I mean...any difficulty breathing? Vision issues?"

"Oh...are you worried about his toxin killing me?" Paige's heart seized in her chest and where moments before she wasn't having difficulty breathing, now she found that she was.

"Nope, not this particular variety of scorpion. That's not to say you couldn't have an allergic reaction though. Any other incidents that you know of? You respond to bee stings or anything like that?"

"No, nothing out of the normal." Paige schooled her breathing, now that she knew there wasn't some weird neurotoxin creeping through her veins about to take her down.

"Then I think we just clean it and bandage you up."

Paige stayed silent for a moment, and watched Jack as he competently cleaned the wound and bandaged her foot. His hands felt cool against her skin, and his touch was sending delicious little tendrils of warmth through her body. If Horatio had found her with a scorpion, he would've gone running for the hills and made someone else handle it. Instead, here Jack was to help her. It was an unusual feeling for Paige, to let someone else tend to her, and she couldn't help but warm to Jack even more for his help.

"Thanks for taking care of me," Paige said.

"No problem. That's what I'm here for."

"What happens if a guest gets hurt? Are you the first responder?"

"I am. As are our security guards and several other staff members. We can handle most minor issues until we can get medical help."

"That's good to know."

"So, you're all patched up now." Jack patted her calf and, looking up, he shot her a smile that made her want to close the door to her office and show him how thankful she was for his assistance. Instead, Paige gingerly pulled her foot off of his lap.

"Thank you."

"Here, let me help you up." Jack hopped easily to his feet and gave her his hand. Hauling her up, he held her arm while she gingerly tested her weight on her foot.

"Oh, it's not so bad anymore."

"Yeah, they have a nasty sting, but it should go away in a day or so."

"Is there any way to scorpion-proof my cottage?"

"Not really. But they aren't super common either. I suggest you get in the habit of shaking your shoes out and doing a quick shake of your bedsheets before you climb in at night."

"I thought we discussed not speaking about scorpions in bed?"

Jack laughed and moved toward the door.

"Best to learn these things now. Scorpions like cool and dark places. Leaving your shoes out like that was a lovely invitation for it to curl up for a nap. Next time, put them up on a shelf."

"Right. Shoes on the shelf."

"Or go barefoot."

Paige gave him a look and Jack laughed again.

"Sorry, I still haven't had coffee."

"I'm heading that way myself. Why don't you join me, and I'll make sure you don't topple over from your battle wounds."

"You just told me I would be fine," Paige grumbled. "Now you're worried I'll fall over and die from the sting."

"Come on, crankypants. Let's get you that coffee."

"My first day on the job is not going as I expected. First I flash my boss and then I get viciously attacked by the biggest scorpion this island has ever seen," Paige said as she limped next to Jack to the kitchen.

"Oh, is that how we are retelling the story now?" Jack grinned down at her.

"Naturally."

"Well, my fearless warrior, you've reached your nirvana – coffee is here." Jack held the door to the kitchen open and Paige almost whimpered in gratitude as the scent of coffee and baked goods greeted her.

"Warrior? Why a warrior? Did you attack our new coordinator, Jack?" Martin, the chef, paused from where he was cutting fruit at a long metal industrial kitchen table.

"Of course. I gotta keep them on the defense at all times."

"I had a run-in with a scorpion." Paige spied the carafe of coffee and limped over to the table to pour herself a cup.

"Oh, nasty little beasts." Martin nodded sympathetically at her.

"I'm off." Jack held up his own mug of coffee to wave goodbye as he headed for the door. "Let me know if there's any lingering effects."

"I will. Thanks for the first-aid."

"No problem."

"You got any lingering effects…for that?" Martin nodded to where Jack had just been standing.

"For…oh, you mean for Jack? Of course not." Paige laughed and buried her face in her coffee.

"Mmhmm. Well, I'm sorry you got stung. But I'm glad you're here. We need to discuss your menu."

"Wait, *what*? My menu?"

"Yes, *your* menu. Apparently, they don't trust me to come up with it on my own." Chef shook his head sadly.

"Wait, why? That's silly. You're the chef."

"That's what I tell them, dear. They don't listen. They say that I don't understand these fancy guests. What's to understand? Food is love. You give love to people. It's very simple."

"Is there like a…detox program or something with the retreat? I don't remember reading about that when we signed up. If so, that's pretty easy – just lemon water or green juices for a few days."

"They *say* they want healthy. But nobody wants healthy on vacation. Two rum punches in and all of a sudden I'm being pulled from bed to put french fries on."

"That sounds about right." Paige laughed. "I'm happy to hand the menu design over to you. You're the expert."

"No good, beauty. You best write it up and I'll make it happen."

"Tell me, what types of food do you like to cook? What's local here?" Paige asked, trying to decide if she should have a muffin. They certainly looked good, but even looking at carbs made her already well-padded hips thicken. That being said, if any a morning called for carbs – it was this one.

"I like delicious comfort food with a lot of heat. We can do seafood, grilled vegetables, all the seasoned rice… that kind of thing."

"That all sounds great. Knowing the Californians, they'll stick their nose up at any carbs, so you'll want to focus on proteins and veggies."

"Fine by me, hermosa. You just need to tell me what to do."

"I'll need help in knowing how much to order. I have no idea what gets wasted or how much to serve."

"No problem. I've got you."

"I'll…" Screw it, Paige needed that muffin now. "I'll just take this to my desk and check in with you once I've got my head wrapped around everything."

"Good luck." Martin laughed. "You'll need it."

"So I hear."

CHAPTER TEN

"What do you mean, there's no tab? I was told there would be a tab for Tranquila Inn here?" Paige gaped at the man at the register at the open-air market she'd found once she'd ventured into town to get the lay of the land.

The ride there had been tricky at best.

Earlier that afternoon, CeCe had handed her the keys to a battered little two-door Suzuki, and told her to head to town to get started. She insisted that Paige have a look around in case guests asked her about activities or restaurants to visit. While Paige agreed that she should have a brief understanding of what Poco Poco Island had to offer, the mountain of paperwork on her desk made her anxious – not to mention she was still limping from her scorpion wound. Despite Paige's protests, CeCe had shooed her away, and that was how Paige had found herself white knuckling the steering wheel of a tiny SUV that she was certain would fall apart at any moment based on the sounds that emanated from beneath the rusted hood. The roads were a mess, and Paige had screeched more than once as she'd swung to avoid a massive pothole and had almost hit an on-coming car. By the time she'd reached town, the back of her dress had been soaked through, and Paige had worked her way through every inventive curse she'd known.

Now, standing here, staring in confusion at the man who shook his head at her, Paige invented a few new iterations of her curse phrases.

"No, señora. No for Tranquila Inn."

"But…" Paige looked down at the tote bag full of fruits she'd gathered. She'd wanted to get a small sampling of what the markets offered before she would work it into the menu. "I was told…"

"No. Tranquila Inn no good."

"How much? Cuánto?" Paige motioned to the bag.

"Twenty. Vente."

"Fine." Paige said and dug the money out of her wallet. She was glad she had some cash on hand or she'd have had to hand the fruit back to the man.

"Do you have a receipt?" she asked, and the man just grinned at her as he took her cash. "Right, got it. No receipt."

Paige took a little notebook from her purse and jotted the expense down, making sure she dated it. She'd need to keep track of everything so that Jack didn't think she was stealing from Tranquila Inn.

Why had the man said that Tranquila Inn was bad? Did he mean their credit was bad? Or the hotel was bad? What was the deal here? The people on the plane had laughed at her as well. Her mind whirling, Paige hefted the tote bag to her shoulder and began to walk through the little downtown.

Clustered on the water were a few blocks of colorful buildings that had been built with little thought to planning or convenience, Paige realized, as she watched traffic try to navigate a confusing mix of side streets that jutted off the main road like little veins. Cars stopped in the middle of the road while their occupants chatted with passersby, and Paige marveled at the fact that nobody in the cars behind them seemed to get angry about it. If it had been California, horns would've been blaring. Instead, people seemed to wait patiently while those in the car ahead of them conducted their conversation and then moved on.

Spying a wellness shop, Paige ducked inside, thinking that perhaps she'd pick up some essential oils or something to use as welcome gifts for the guests at the retreat. She'd already been toying around with the idea of a welcome basket and wanted to source a few items to get an idea of costs.

Paige smiled at the pretty brown-haired woman who stood behind the counter. Moving to a row of wooden shelves decorated with hand-painted flowers, she took her time examining the various jars. Paige let the tension ease from her shoulders as she opened one body scrub to smell the vanilla coconut scent. She was at home here, among the softly playing music, heavenly scents, and natural health care options. Gathering a few items she liked, Paige brought them to the counter.

"Hola. I…do you have a tab for Tranquila Inn here?"

The woman's smile dropped from her face, and she emphatically shook her head.

"No, no. No Tranquila Inn."

"No tab or you won't run a tab for them?"

"No." The woman shook her head again, concern crossing her pretty face. She obviously wanted the sale, but wouldn't do so on credit.

"How much?" Paige asked, the tension returning to her shoulders.

Paige sighed when the woman quoted her a price. Looking at the items she'd gathered, she put back everything except for the body scrub.

"What about this?"

"Five. Cinco." Sympathy lines crossed the woman's face as she took Paige's money.

"Can I ask you why you don't have a tab for Tranquila Inn? Is something wrong with the hotel?"

The woman just looked at her blankly, and Paige realized she spoke limited English.

"Right. Okay, thank you." Smiling, Paige left the little shop, tucking her body scrub into her tote bag. For a moment, she just stood on the sidewalk, unsure of where to go or what to do. The heat pressed against her, and sweat led a sticky trail down her back to her underwear. Her shoulders dropped, and Paige drew in a shaky breath, reminding herself that she would get through this. Her record of survival thus far had been one hundred percent – Horatio's cheating, losing her job, the scary plane ride, a ruthless scorpion attack, Jack's immediate dismissal of her upon arrival...

"You look like you could use a beer."

Paige turned to see Jack leaning against the wall of a shop, a cheeky grin on his face. How did the man manage to look so cool and collected in this heat? He'd thrown on a loose t-shirt with a surfboard design and his eyes were shaded by aviators.

"You know what? I think you're right. Except I'm fairly certain if I drink anything at all, I'll never get that car that's held together by duct tape home."

"Nothing wrong with a little duct tape. It fixes everything, you know." Jack's grin widened.

"Uh-huh." Paige nodded, unconvinced.

"I'll drive you home. I rode in with Luis anyway."

"How were you planning to get back?"

"Taxi. Hitchhike." Jack shrugged his shoulders. "I hadn't thought much of it."

"Hitchhike? Seems like an unnecessary risk."

"Says the woman who flew to an island with an unconfirmed employment offer."

"Touché." Not that Paige needed to be reminded of her questionable decision-making skills.

"So? Shall we have a drink? You look like you could use some refreshment."

"Is that a polite way of saying I'm a sweaty mess?" Paige nodded her thanks when Jack took the tote bag full of food from her shoulder.

"It's the Caribbean. Everyone sweats. You'll get used to it."

"You keep saying that. Where are we going?"

"A little local bar down the way. It's not too far. Turn here." Jack indicated the street ahead of them. "We'll walk on the shady side."

"A small blessing," Paige breathed.

"How's the foot?" Jack asked as he waved at a man

turning churros at a little stand. The scent of cinnamon and sugar made her mouth water.

"It's better. Barely limping."

She kept quiet as Jack waved or nodded at people as they passed. It seemed like he knew everyone. In a matter of moments, they'd arrived at a thatched roof bar with a few rickety looking tables in front of it, situated directly across from the harbor.

"Bar or table?"

"Bar is fine," Paige said, as the tables were still in the sun. She didn't need to peel herself off of the chair when they left. Settling into a stool under the shaded thatch of the bar, Paige flapped the neck of her dress, trying to stir up some air movement.

"You'll get used to the humidity. I promise. Summers are hot here though, and nobody is really immune to it."

Jack held up two fingers and Paige didn't even bother to tell him she didn't like beer. Right then, she'd drink sewer water if it was cold. Well, maybe not that, but still... when the beers arrived in a little bucket of ice, Paige reached in and grabbed a cube to run down the back of her neck. The cold was intense against her skin, but immediately began to relieve some of the heat that pressed against her.

"Why are the beers so tiny? They are like half the size of a bottle in the States." Paige peered into the bucket.

"So the beer stays cold as you drink it. Otherwise beer runs to warm real fast here."

"Ah."

"Cheers." Jack tapped his beer to hers and Paige drank. It wasn't half bad, she realized, and perhaps that was the missing component to enjoying beer – it just needed to be ice cold and she needed to be desperately hot.

"Jack…what's going on here? CeCe told me there would be tabs at the shops in town. But nobody would let me use them. Is it the language barrier?"

"Yeah. That." Jack pressed his lips together and looked away for a moment. Paige studied his face as he worked out what he was going to say. He might possibly be one of the most handsome men she'd ever seen – but in a rough and tumble sort of way. There were a lot of really good-looking men in California, but most of them had a polished sheen to them. Jack was all man with rough edges. He was like raw quartz compared to perfectly tumbled round quartz stones. Both were appealing in their own way.

"Yes, that?" Paige pushed.

"I'm doing my best to restore our reputation in town." Jack finished a mini beer and reached for another.

"Because the last coordinator stole?"

"Partly."

It didn't take long for Paige to realize the other problem.

"CeCe?"

Jack gave a curt nod.

"Spending more than they have?"

"It's not even that. CeCe and Whit are loaded. It's just that they are absent-minded. Or, if I'm being honest – irresponsible. It was why the last coordinator could steal so easily from us. However, unreliable doesn't work well on an island that relies on word-of-mouth reputation for getting things done. The thing is…many people here… Well, they are working paycheck to paycheck. That cash you gave for your fruit? It goes straight home to pay the rent or pay for their family or extended family. Since I've taken over accounts, people are starting to trust us again, but it's a slow process to restore our reputation. It's not cheap to live on an island, and much is imported here. Housing prices can reflect that. Same with cars. You wonder why the Suzuki is strung together with bits and pieces?"

"I'm guessing parts are hard to come by?"

"Hard to come by *and* expensive. Sometimes parts take months to get here. You get used to it." Jack shrugged.

"I'm beginning to see that there is a lot to adjust to with island life."

"More than you can imagine. Welcome to the ride, sweets."

CHAPTER ELEVEN

"I might not be tall enough to ride this ride," Paige said, keeping her tone light.

Jack looked to where her feet swung from the bar stool, mirth in his eyes, before shaking his head and taking a long pull from his beer. "Looks like you're on it either way."

"Lucky me," Paige said, but shot Jack a smile to soften her words. "But in all seriousness, it is good for me to have a challenge to tackle. A bit of pressure is always something that keeps me in line. Forces me to focus. Hone in on what needs to get done."

"Not one to fall apart when a deadline looms?" Jack asked.

"Nope. I like it. Otherwise I can end up starting a gazillion little projects and not finishing any."

"What kind of projects?"

"Hmm, that's a good question." Paige leaned back against the rough wood back of the stool and stared out to the water. It had been so long since she'd done anything that wasn't expressly related to Yoga Soulone. She was just now realizing how much the studio and Horatio had dominated her life. "I used to like to paint, but it's been ages since I've picked up a brush."

"What kind of things did you paint?"

"Watercolors mostly. I'd go down to the beach in Santa Cruz and watch the surfers. Try to capture the light of the sun on the water. I don't suppose I was any good at it. But I enjoyed it. I enjoyed that time to myself," Paige admitted as she took another drink of her beer. Holding it up, she was surprised to find the clear glass bottle empty.

"Why did you stop then?" Jack grabbed another bottle for her and cranked the neck of it in a little bottle opener stuck to the side of the bucket.

"Oh, well, I never had time for it after I went to work for the studio. It seemed like there was always something to be done and I was the one who had to handle it."

"Why didn't this Horatio guy handle some of it?"

"Oh, he couldn't be bothered to do that. He had to focus on his teaching." Resentment roiled in her stomach at her words and when the silence drew out, Paige realized how it sounded to Jack. "Okay, right. I get it."

"Do you?" Jack laughed. "Listen, we've all had our share of bad relationships. Sounds to me like this guy wanted you to run his business for cheap."

"I was paid," Paige said stiffly.

"Sounds like he was getting a hell of a deal – sex and business manager."

"I will smash this over your head." Paige held up her beer bottle and glared at Jack.

"Bloodthirsty little one, aren't ya?" Instead of admonishing her for her anger, Jack just laughed, which helped ease the tension that knotted her gut.

"I'm sorry," Paige said, grinning at him. "I'm not sure I'm quite ready to put my ex-relationship under a microscope. You're certainly right. I gave more than I should've for my job and my...well, I guess he wasn't *my* boyfriend. Apparently, he was *everyone's* boyfriend."

"A true renaissance man," Jack said and Paige surprised herself by snorting.

"A man of the people," Paige snickered.

"Lives by the motto: what's mine is yours."

"His penis: free to a good home." Paige doubled over in laughter, the first time she'd really laughed this hard in she didn't know how long.

"A real winner, this Horatio." Jack patted her lightly on the back as she gasped for air. "Feeling better?"

"Oh..." Paige gasped and wiped tears from her eyes. "It feels so good to make fun of him. I had no idea I had that in me. Everyone always spoke in hushed tones about him and like bowed to him as though he was some Greek god or something. But he isn't...not at all. He's just an excellent manipulator."

"It certainly sounds that way. Is he any good at teaching yoga?"

"Ah..." Paige sat back and took another sip of her cold beer as she thought about it. A light breeze had moved in, cooling the sweat at her back, and people flowed past on their way to the harbor. "You know what? He wasn't always bad. I learned a lot about poses and what-not from him. But he shamed people into trying to get into more difficult poses when he should have helped them with props and stuff like that. We had a lot of injuries because of it."

"That doesn't sound healthy. I'm surprised people didn't push back."

"But that's the pull of him. He convinced them it was their fault and they never realized they could've learned the stepping-stones into a pose. I had one woman who broke her nose doing a crow pose because she'd never been told that she could use blocks to learn the pose first."

"What?" Jack looked at her in surprise. "That sounds really violent. And what is crow pose?"

"Um, it's…" Paige looked around but realized there was no way she was going to demonstrate crow pose on the dirty cement pavement around the bar. "It's a pose where you balance your knees on the backs of your arms."

"I see and so once you get your knees on the back of your arms?"

"You should be able to sit there."

"And if you pitch yourself too far forward…" Jack made a flat motion with his hand and then tipped it forward.

"Splat," Paige said.

"So she really broke her nose, huh?"

"She did. It was awful. In theory she should have just dropped to the side and caught herself, but the woman was very determined to impress Horatio."

"What did he do?"

"He assured her that she would get it on the next try."

"Ooof."

"Ooof is right." Paige shook her head sadly, but also

realized what a relief it was not to have to be cleaning up Horatio's messes anymore.

"I'll admit I've been a bit worried about how you are going to handle the retreat once I found out your relationship to this group."

"Is that why you came to find me?

"That and I wanted to make sure you weren't boarding the next flight out of here."

"Oh, have no worries about that." Paige finished her beer. "I haven't been paid yet. I couldn't afford to if I wanted to."

Jack burst out laughing, and Paige joined him, even though it was the truth. Shoot, if she couldn't laugh at the situations she got herself into, then what was the damn point of it all?

CHAPTER TWELVE

P aige leaned back against the cracked upholstery of the passenger seat of the little Suzuki, not caring that vinyl stuck to the back of her legs so long as she didn't have to try to navigate driving stick shift and narrow pothole-filled roads. They'd finished happy hour on a good note, and Paige was feeling relaxed as they left the little downtown and headed toward Tranquila Inn.

"So, before Yoga Soulone…what did you do? Or have you always been a devout yogi?" Jack shot her a look as he shifted gears as the Suzuki approached a hill. Paige tilted her face into the breeze that whipped through the windows and thought about his question.

"Well, I've bounced around a lot, I suppose. I've always enjoyed yoga, but didn't do my teacher training until I started at Yoga Soulone. Prior to that, I worked as an events coordinator for a large banquet hall in Santa Cruz for years before I got let go when the economy took a hit. That's how I ended up at the studio. I wanted a job that would keep me active and around people."

"Not a desk job type of girl?"

"God, no. I tried it, actually, for years. I worked as a legal secretary for my father's law firm. It didn't go well, to say the least, and I think they kept me on more out of pity than anything after my father passed away."

"I'm sorry."

"Don't be. He was a dick."

Jack jerked his head around and then laughed.

"Well, then why did you work for him?"

"An easy job out of college. I think a part of me still wanted to please him, I guess. But, in all reality, we were oil and water. He'd always wanted me to be a boy. Then my name could be on the letterhead along with his. Women weren't good enough to share the title of partner."

"Sounds…well, it sounds pretty shitty, I'd say."

"It was. I'm over it. What about you?"

"What about me?" Jack shrugged one shoulder.

"How'd you end up here? Driving a rickety car on a tiny island in the Caribbean?"

"I'm originally from Connecticut."

"Oh an East Coast boy. Got it."

"What do you mean by that?"

"You guys have a reputation. You know…like to yacht. Love the Yankees. Uptight."

A smile cracked Jack's handsome face.

"I'll give you most of that except the yachting. I prefer a sailboat, thank you very much."

"Naturally. So how did a Connecticut boy end up at Tranquila Inn with his shirt off and covered in dirt?"

"I took hospitality management in college. From there I bounced around the world working internships and jobs at every level of the hotel management industry. I learned pretty quickly that you have to know how everything runs in order to actually manage a hotel properly. So, you'd better be just as comfortable fixing a toilet as you are greeting royalty."

"Hence the Jack of all trades…"

"Exactly."

"And now you're here. Rescuing Tranquila Inn."

"Precisely."

"I see…" Paige nodded. "So…Luis and Martin are awesome. But…"

"CeCe and Whit?" Jack asked, glancing at her with a quick smile of understanding as he shifted gears as they wound along the cliffs next to the water.

"Any tips there? Insights?"

"Don't go on any long walks with Whit and don't go one-for-one with drinks with CeCe."

"Um…" Paige's mouth dropped open as she tried to figure out a diplomatic way to respond to that.

"They'll grow on you. They're relatively harmless and they are more obsessed with the images they project to have than actual reality."

"Okay…" Paige's voice rose on a questioning note.

"In other words…don't try to babysit or manage them as they'll do exactly what they want, when they want. It's kind of like herding incorrigible toddlers. You're better to just treat them as entertainment. They're surprisingly great with guests and you'll see that most people will fall under their weird brand of charm. When it comes to running a business? It's a shitshow. Consult me on all business matters. Don't let CeCe make any decisions though as she'll constantly try to implement them. And, yeah...that's your basic rundown," Jack said.

"Right, okay." Paige blew out a breath and rubbed her sweaty palms on her thighs. "So, off to the races?"

"Pretty much. Don't screw it up."

"Gee...thanks." Paige glared at him and Jack laughed as he brought the Suzuki to a shuddering stop.

"You'll love it or hate it. That much I can promise."

Paige's eyebrows shot up as the engine of the car made a weird cranking noise and then the whole frame began to shudder. Panic lanced through her and she grabbed the support handle on the dashboard of the Suzuki as Jack eased the car over and brought it to a halting stop on the side of the dusty road.

"What happened?" Paige gasped, looking wildly around.

"Duct tape must've failed."

CHAPTER THIRTEEN

"I thought you were joking about the duct tape." Paige pushed down on the tendrils of panic that felt like a vise tightening on her throat.

"Partly." Jack hummed as he got out of the car and moved easily to the hood.

Paige took a deep breath. And then another. It was her fault, really. Hadn't she asked if this day could get any worse? Now, here they were, stranded on the side of a busted-up road and the light was steadily disappearing. Soon, they'd be in full darkness.

The little SUV rocked as Jack opened the creaky hood, and Paige blinked through the front windshield at the rusted metal that now blocked her view. Surely, he'd be able to fix this, right?

Paige jumped as Jack slammed the hood down.

"Not much I can do, I'm afraid."

"Wait. What? I thought you were the Jack of all trades?"

Jack shot Paige a smile as he wiped his hands on his shorts.

"Yes, and master of none. This falls outside the scope of my capabilities."

"But…but…now what? Can you call for help?"

"With what?" Jack looked around at the prickly bushes that surrounded the road.

"You don't have a cell phone?" Paige looked at him as if he'd just confessed he'd murdered a prostitute in Rio and taken her money to run the tables all night.

"Not with me."

"But…why? How? You just go to town without one? What if someone needs you? Or you need something?"

"People know how to get to town to find me." Jack shrugged.

Paige glanced at the darkening sky as fear began to work its way up her spine.

"How will we get home? It's not safe here. People won't be able to see us. What if we get jumped? Can you call Triple A?" Paige realized she was babbling as Jack just steadily looked at her.

"There's no Triple A."

"And you have no phone anyway. Oh. God." Paige suddenly remembered her own tote and she dug hastily in it. "Wait! I have a phone!"

"Good luck with that." Jack quirked a smile at her and waited patiently until she located the phone and brandished it like a trophy to him.

"See? Here you go. Call someone for help."

Jack took the phone and looked at it before handing it back to Paige.

"What?"

"No service."

"But…" Paige looked down at the screen to see he was right. "How can there possibly be no service? Everywhere has service. Is that even a thing anymore?"

"Not everywhere has service." Jack outright laughed at her this time and Paige looked up at him, stricken.

"No service. No working phone. No car. No light. Oh my god. We're going to die out here."

"And here I was beginning to think you were somewhat levelheaded. Come on, sweets. Let's go." Jack rounded the car and opened the door. Paige looked blankly at him.

"Go? Go where? You want us to walk?"

"Until we see a car, yes. Or, if we don't, then we'll walk to Tranquila."

"How far is that?"

"Mmm, maybe a few more miles or so?" Jack shrugged.

"Lovely. What about if we see a car? People will stop to help us, right?"

"Like I said… they'll give us a ride."

"Hitchhiking?" Paige shook her head in disbelief. "I thought you were joking about that."

"Nope."

Paige stared at him. "That's how people get murdered."

"Maybe so." Jack laughed. "But highly unlikely here. It's hard to get away with murder on a small island. Not saying it's impossible, just unlikely. And usually I just hop in the back of a pick-up truck so I never even really talk to the person."

"Without a seatbelt? You want me to just hop in the back?"

"Paige. Get out of the car." Jack's patience seemed to be drying up and Paige finally realized she was not helping the situation. He was absolutely right – the sooner they started walking, the sooner they'd get home. Blowing out a breath, Paige nodded to the bag in the back.

"You're carrying the fruit."

"That's fine."

They plodded along the road in silence for a while, Jack schooling his pace to hers as she was still limping slightly from her scorpion sting that morning. The last traces of the sunset streaked across the sky and aside from the occasional squawk of a bird settling for the night, the road was quiet. A gentle breeze kicked up the dust as they walked, and Paige tried her best not to fall into her anxiety.

"If you could have any superpower what would it be?" Jack surprised her from her worries with his question.

"What? A Superpower?"

"Sure, like…flying or lasers shooting from your butt."

"In what world is lasers shooting from your butt a superpower? Paige shook her head at Jack. The palm leaves rustled softly as they continued their walk, navigating as best they could around potholes in the waning light.

"I mean, I'm pretty sure that's every dude's choice of a superpower. Could you imagine how fast you could clear out a buffet line?"

"Wouldn't a normal fart also accomplish the same feat?" Paige asked.

"Hmm, the woman has a point."

Paige rolled her eyes. "I think I'd like to be a mermaid. There's something so enchanting about the idea of swimming underwater."

"And luring men to their deaths. There's more of that bloodthirst, I see."

Paige found herself laughing. "Maybe the mermaids were never interested in luring men, perhaps they were just trying to have their own space. One where humans didn't interfere."

"Then why was it always men that were killed?"

"Because they were the ones dumb enough to think every beautiful woman, errr… half-woman, would be instantly attracted to them? I swear the male ego…" Paige sighed.

"Oh, for sure it gets us in trouble. I won't argue with you on that." Jack laughed, and the sound warmed her.

"Thanks, Jack." Paige realized he'd been trying to distract her from the anxiety that had threatened to overtake her at being caught unprepared on the side of the dark road.

"Why does this bother you so much?" Jack asked, looking down at her. He'd moved around her to the outside, so that he was more in the road, and she was walking along the bush side.

"The car breaking down? I mean, it sucks, right?"

"Sure, but you genuinely seemed like you were about to panic there for a moment."

"I…" Paige considered his words. "I guess it goes back to that feeling of safety we talked about last night. It just felt so out of my comfort zone. All of my solutions for that car breaking down are based on things that aren't valid here. My phone doesn't work. No roadside assistance. No freaking duct tape."

At that, Jack threw back his head and laughed, and despite her mood, Paige found her lips quirking in response.

"It's good to leave your bubble. You learn new things. And you'll learn different ways to solve your problems."

"I guess, if it had been me on my own, I'd have been even more scared. But I feel better that you're with me." Paige met his eyes and the look held for a moment before a flash of light from ahead washed over them.

"I won't let anything happen to you," Jack promised and stepping forward, he raised an arm. "And, I'm about to teach you a new and island-tested solution for when your car breaks down."

A truck that looked as destined for the landfill as their Suzuki slowed to a stop.

"Hey, Jack." The driver nodded. "Got a problem?"

"Our car's broken down. Can you drop us at Tranquila?"

"No problemo. But the cab's full. Hop in the back."

"Thanks, Manuel."

The driver nodded and Paige gaped when Jack rounded the back of the truck and held out his hand to her.

"But there's no seatbelts…"

Jack just grinned at her and she took his hand.

"I've got you, Paige. You're gonna be just fine."

CHAPTER FOURTEEN

"They sound crazy."

"Oh. They are. Or not. I can't decide yet," Paige was digging through the small closet where she'd hung her clothes. "Maybe they have it all figured out? And have not a care in the world?"

"Maybe. I'll need to be updated regularly," Jane said. Her friend had narrowed in on CeCe and Whit, demanding more information on their shenanigans.

She'd called Jane first thing the next morning before the impending arrival of Yoga Soulone's group. Paige was grateful for a familiar voice to debrief about what had happened since she'd arrived on Poco Poco Island. While Paige felt some uncertainty with her situation, they'd both agreed that her current state of affairs certainly wasn't boring. So there was that, Paige thought, as she pulled a deep blue dress from the closet. It was kind of like bungee jumping – there was a chance this could all go really really badly, but at the same time the adrenaline rush was fun.

"How am I going to face Horatio?" Paige changed the subject to more important matters.

"Like the badass you are?" Jane asked. Briefly she turned her mouth from the phone and shouted something unintelligible to a child behind her. There were a few screams and then silence settled. "Listen, I know I only saw you for a brief, chaotic moment before you hopped a plane to wherever the hell you are. But you didn't seem at all like a woman that was heartbroken about losing her man. You kept talking about all you'd done for the studio. So is it really the man you're upset about losing or your job?"

Paige paused at that.

"I…okay, I'll admit I was really proud of my job. I liked what I did and I thought I was good at it. And with Horatio…"

"How many hours of sleep have you lost over him since you left? A broken-hearted woman stays up obsessing over the man she lost. Be honest." Another crash sounded in the background behind Jane.

"I…well, none," Paige admitted. "My pride's hurt, I suppose. I should've known better or seen the signs."

"That's a victim mentality. *He* lied to you. That's on him. Full stop. You did nothing wrong. You can hold your head high and know you did a good job running his business and were a respectful partner to him. You have nothing to be ashamed of here, Paige. It's Horatio who should be embarrassed when he sees you."

"I don't think he even knows that emotion." Paige couldn't remember Horatio ever being embarrassed.

"Well, just hold your head high. Look at you now!

You've left a little studio and are running events for a hotel on a tropical island. I think you're the real winner here. Plus, you don't have to look at his stupid man bun anymore."

Paige snorted. "It was kind of dumb, wasn't it?"

"God, I wanted to pull it on more than one occasion. I'm just glad that I get to say that out loud now. What is he…like mid-thirties and rocking a man bun?"

"I mean…it fits his look, I guess."

"It's stupid. I gotta go. The middle child has discovered the laundry soap."

"I love you. Thanks for the stern talking to. I needed some mothering today."

"Call me anytime. I'm happy to kick you in the ass whenever you need it."

"Is that what good moms do? I wouldn't know," Paige laughed.

"Yes, they boot you in the ass when you're being dumb and then they hug you and make you a grilled cheese. I can only metaphorically do those things for you, so instead I'll tell you I love you and I know you've got this. Make me proud, girl."

"Love you, too," Paige said, but Jane was already gone, presumably to stop her child from drinking soap. Even if she wasn't used to being mothered, the pep talk felt good. She had always been able to rely on Jane for good advice.

"You have nothing to be ashamed of," Paige repeated to herself. "No need to slink away and hide." She put the blue dress back and instead pulled out a silky pink number that was more figure hugging. Large hibiscus flowers in red were splashed across the fabric in a fun tropical print. It was a dress she wore when she wanted to feel pretty and powerful and what better time than now? She slid a jeweled headband on her head to pull her hair off her face and let her curls tumble down her back. Tucking simple silver hoops in her ears, Paige stopped in front of the mirror and studied her face. A few days in the sun, even though she'd been largely in the office or running about, had kissed her cheeks with a touch of color. Deciding against any makeup, Paige grabbed her tote full of folders, her laptop, and cell phone, and left her cottage ready to handle whatever came her way.

"Damn, mama..." Luis whistled from where he trimmed the branch of a plumeria tree. "You are looking spicy today."

"Too much?" Paige paused in front of him and twirled.

"What are you going for?"

"My ex-boyfriend and his mistresses are in the group arriving today."

"Then you look perfect. Just sexy enough, but in charge, you know? Like you belong here. This island might be good for you, mama."

"You think? I hope so. Oh, I loved your idea about the flower necklaces you mentioned at dinner yesterday. Do you think it would be too much trouble?"

"I already started on them. They'll be done by the time the group arrives." Luis gestured to where a bucket of flowers sat at his feet. "I like that you are open to my ideas."

"Are you kidding me? You have great ideas! I mean, you keep this garden looking amazing. I'm always happy to listen to any suggestions you have. I'm new here, so I will take any help or advice, too."

"You're a good one, mama. I'll make you a special flower necklace, okay?"

"I'd appreciate that. Oh, what did you think of my ideas for the welcome packs?"

"It's good. Not too much, but just enough. The local body scrub is nice. Along with a pretty sarong? They'll love it."

"Good, that's what I'm going for. Classy, but not breaking the bank."

"Nailed it. Good luck with the ex. Let me know which one he is. I'll put the eye on him." Luis made a complicated motion with his fingers. Paige didn't want to ask more about what the "eye" was, but nodded before giving him a little wave and continuing on her way to the office. She still had a million things to do and had made lists upon lists. Well, not really a *million*, but it would still make her feel better to run through the programs and make sure everything was just the way she wanted it to be. Nerves hummed low in her stomach, but she rode the wave of anxiety through the morning as she worked and kept an eye on the flight arrival information to make sure the plane would be on time. Once Paige saw that the flight had landed, she took a few deep centering breaths, and closed her laptop.

"You're gonna nail this, Paige. Fuck Horatio," Paige said out loud to herself.

"Well, I hope that's not how you greet him."

Paige's eyes popped open and her hand flew to her mouth.

"I…oh, god, Jack. You scared me."

"Having a little pep talk, were you?"

"You weren't supposed to hear that."

"Just so long as Horatio doesn't hear that, I don't really care."

"He won't. I promise. That was my baser side coming out. Dark energy stuck in my chakras and all that, as Horatio would say."

"Well, we'll have to figure out how to work that energy out." Jack gave Paige a slow grin that set off a flash of heat low in her stomach. "Just not on Horatio. From this moment on, he is nothing to you but a guest – our primary guest. Understood?"

"You don't have to worry about me."

Jack looked her up and down.

"You're looking very nice today."

"I thought I'd dress up to greet the guests."

"For what it's worth, I think you've done a great job so far and I think we're lucky to have you. This is Horatio's loss and our gain." With that, Jack disappeared from her office door as quickly as he'd arrived.

Huh, Paige thought, as she pressed a hand to her solar plexus. Maybe Jack had actually helped move the dark energy out – perhaps not in the way he'd insinuated, but his words had been like a cool balm to the fire of her anger. Now, she threw her shoulders back, stuck her chin in the air, and went to greet the new guests.

Just guests, she reminded herself. She could do this in her sleep.

CeCe and Whit had assumed their usual positions at the bar, and Paige hoped that they hadn't gone too deep into their martinis. She had yet to come up with her strategy for how she'd deal with them when it came to guests. Remembering Jack's assurance that they were surprisingly good with the clientele, she had decided to do her best to try not to control every aspect and would let the experience unfold as it would. CeCe looked sexy in a fitted mint green wrap dress that hugged her curves and a braided silver and gold twist of a necklace at her throat. Whit had boat shoes, pressed linen shorts, and a Bermuda shirt on. Paige wondered who was pressing their clothes – was there even a dry cleaner on the island? She couldn't imagine CeCe or Whit getting up every morning and ironing their outfits for the day.

When a sharp wolf whistle pierced the air, they both turned to look at Paige as she approached them. Paige laughed at Martin who waved to her from across the reception hall where he was setting out welcome snacks.

"Paige, you look gorgeous. Simply gorgeous," CeCe trilled and came forward to air kiss her on both cheeks.

"That Horatio is going to eat his tongue when he sees you," Whit agreed. Paige sighed and wondered if she had been smart to share her personal story with everyone. Too late now, she thought, and glanced to where Mariposa had joined the group behind the bar. Her mouth dropped open.

If Paige looked pretty, then Mariposa looked positively decadent. The bartender wore a simple white halter style dress that hugged every inch of her generous curves. The white made her dusky skin glow, and she'd slicked her hair back into a sleek knot and hung large turquoise drops from her ears. Some trick of eyeshadow made her eyes look luminous in her face and if Paige wasn't firmly in the heterosexual camp, she'd be ready to switch teams just looking at Mariposa.

"Wow, Mariposa. You look fantastic," Paige breathed. Mariposa flashed her a wide smile.

"Americans like to tip." Mariposa shrugged a shoulder.

"I suspect you'll make a killing. You look like you should be on the cover of a magazine," Paige said. She watched as Mariposa lined up a row of tiki glasses, each mug done in a different color and character. "What are you making?"

"Just a welcome rum punch. It loosens people up when they are hot and sweaty from travel. Most people arrive here stressed. A little rum punch helps them chill out."

"Good idea. Save one of these for me at the end of the night."

"You got it."

"They're here in twenty," Luis called from across the reception hall where he was laying out flower necklaces. "Miquel texted me from the airport. They're on the bus."

"Perfect. Just enough time for a quick tipple," CeCe said and reached to where a martini had appeared for her at the bar. Paige did her best to disguise her look, but CeCe caught it. "Don't worry, darling. I'm an old hand at this. I won't be the one you have to worry about."

With that, CeCe sipped her drink as the bartender turned the music on the overhead speakers louder.

"Don't worry…about a thing…"

But now all Paige could do was wonder who she really needed to worry about?

CHAPTER FIFTEEN

The look on Horatio's face was priceless.

Actually, Paige was having a hard time deciding which looks were better – Horatio's frozen mask or Nadia and Lily's shocked and murderous expressions when they saw her at the front of the reception hall. Paige's nerves quickly disappeared, and she found herself enjoying the moment. Pasting a bright smile on her face, she moved forward with Luis, strands of flower necklaces hanging from her arms.

"Welcome. Namaste," Paige repeated over and over as people recognized her and said hello.

There were thirty people total in the group, and Paige knew most of the guests by name already. She'd sorted them into cabins based on their personalities and well-established friendships. Some of the guests were happy to see her, while others looked between her and Horatio in confusion. She wondered what story he'd told people about her departure from the studio. The only two who refused to greet her were Nadia and Lily, and she was more than happy to pass them over to Luis for their flower garlands.

"Paige, what a surprise." Horatio stopped in front of her, and Paige handed him a flower necklace which he slipped over his neck.

"Horatio. I trust your flight was pleasant?" Paige kept her tone smooth and stayed in customer service mode.

"It was, yes. As pleasant as flying can be, I suppose. Is there a reason you are on this...retreat?" Horatio glanced around the open reception hall and then back to Paige. He looked...well, exactly like a mid-thirties yoga guru should look, Paige supposed. She was surprised not to feel a tug of anything for him except a brief flash of annoyance that she'd wasted several years with this man. Horatio's hair was tucked in his typical man bun, and he wore a long flowing tunic in beige, and loose striped pants beneath the tunic. Beaded bracelets jumbled together at his wrists and several hemp necklaces were clustered around his throat.

"I'm not on the retreat," Paige clarified. "I'm running it." She smiled sweetly at Horatio and was rewarded when a hot flash of anger zipped across his face before he schooled his features again. Gotta work on those chakras, Horatio, Paige thought to herself and bit back a smug smile.

"Is that so? How convenient, I'm sure."

"I'd say so. Since I already know all the guests, I've been able to tailor much of the programming to their specific needs."

"Won't I be running the retreat?" Again, the flash of anger. My, my, Paige thought. This man did not like being out of control. Interesting how she had always accepted it without question before.

"No, you're here for a retreat run by Tranquila Inn. We've meticulously designed the programming to suit our guests' needs. Speaking of, you'll likely want to get settled. We've arranged for all of the guests to be in their shared cottages. I've got your cottage over here along with your roommates."

"Roommates?" Horatio glanced at her as he walked to the table where folders and keys were laid out. "I didn't expect to share."

"Ah, yes, seeing as how we understand you adhere strongly to an open-door policy, we've grouped everyone in their cottages in what we hope will be enjoyable pairings." Horatio shot her another sharp look, but Paige kept her customer service smile pasted on her face. She was *really* beginning to enjoy this. "You'll see that you're in cottage number three. This is one of our most well-appointed cottages with lovely ocean views."

"And my...roommates?" Horatio sniffed as he took the key from Paige.

"Horatio! We're with you!" Nadia and Lily scampered over to Horatio and turned their backs on Paige. She wasn't surprised they refused to speak to her, but the look on Horatio's face was worth every moment of stress she'd felt leading up to their arrival. Horatio looked askance at the two women who all but clambered over themselves to reach him. Paige wondered what had happened to his open-door policy? From his expression, it looked like Horatio wanted nothing to do with the two bendy yogis she'd recently discovered in bed with him.

"Luis will show you to your cottage. There's a welcome reception in this hall tonight. You'll have time to rest and rejuvenate before then. All of the information you need is in your folders and your welcome gifts are in the room. Namaste." Paige faded away before Horatio could ask her anything else, and Luis stepped forward to gesture to the group to follow him. Luis shot Paige a questioning glance, and she winked and nodded to Horatio. Luis rolled his eyes behind Horatio's back and made a quick gagging gesture before Horatio turned back and Luis beamed at him.

Paige suppressed a giggle and quickly greeted a few friendly regulars who gave her hugs before everyone disappeared to find their cottages or wandered to the bar. Happy voices filled the reception hall, and Paige took a few deep breaths. It hadn't been as bad as she'd feared, though she was certain that she'd be dealing with a difficult Horatio as he adjusted to not being in control.

"I'm presuming you didn't tell Horatio to…" Jack came to her, and Paige gave him a sharp look to stop what he was going to say.

"I most certainly did not." Paige laughed.

"You look a little too pleased with yourself. What did you say?"

"It appears he thought he would be in his own cabin."

"Isn't the description clear about shared cottages on the retreat info?" Jack's forehead furrowed in confusion.

"It is. But Horatio likes to be in charge. So I reminded him of his open-door policy and roomed him with two of his favorites."

"Let me guess…the women you found him with?"

"Correct. I figured why bother separating them and having them sneak around when they can just stay in the same cottage and enjoy themselves?"

"You are entirely too cheerful about this. I take it Horatio didn't share your enthusiasm?"

"Let's just say he looked less than pleased with his cabin buddies."

"Trouble in paradise already? This should be interesting." A wide grin split Jack's face and Paige laughed again. Turning, she caught an unreadable look that Mariposa sent them before the bartender bent her head to mix more drinks for a few people who had stopped by the bar.

CeCe's raucous laugh reverberated through the main hall, and Paige decided to cross to the bar to run interference. But when she got there, she found Whit detailing the best areas to go snorkeling and CeCe advising a guest about how to keep looking fresh in the humidity. Okay, so maybe things wouldn't be so bad after all, Paige thought.

"I'll take that rum punch now," Paige said.

"Let me make you a normal one," Mariposa whispered from the side of her mouth.

Bending closer, Paige looked at her in confusion.

"What's an abnormal one?" Paige asked in hushed tones.

"For the guests, I put four extra shots in. Trust me. It works wonders."

Paige's eyebrows rose as she realized that all of the tiki cups were gone and that many of the guests had disappeared to their cottages. Hoping the extra alcohol would knock them out for the afternoon, she took another deep breath and accepted the mug Mariposa offered her.

"I made it extra light. Just enough to take the edge off, but you'll be fine for work."

"Have I mentioned that you're a goddess?"

"Nope. But keep doing so. I accept all forms of flattery."

With that, Mariposa went back to mix a drink for another guest, chattering more than Paige had ever seen her talk before.

Feeling at ease for the first time in days, Paige took a sip of her rum punch and steadied herself. So far, the worst of her fears had been alleviated and nothing major had gone wrong. If she could just keep a tight hold of the reins, she might be able to get through the next three weeks with a modicum of ease.

Err...or not. Paige quickly set her drink down as Horatio stormed across the reception hall, Lily trailing behind him. In his hand was the Welcome Folder she'd given to each guest.

"Paige!" Horatio barked and everyone quickly quieted as he approached, brandishing the folder in the air.

"Yes, Horatio? Is there something that I can help you with?" Paige kept her tone light and even, as though she was soothing a rattlesnake that looked ready to bite.

"I don't know who wrote this schedule, but it's absolutely wrong."

"I wrote the schedule, Horatio." Whit and CeCe both managed to cover their looks of displeasure at a public confrontation. "What seems to be the issue?"

"There's no sunrise meditation tomorrow. You know I always like to do a sunrise meditation," Horatio insisted.

"Yeah, Paige. Horatio needs his spiritual time. How

could you cut that out?" Lily said, her hand on a hip and head tilted in accusation.

What Paige knew was that Horatio loved *telling* people about his sunrise meditations. However, unless he had a class scheduled at sunrise, Horatio was never out of bed before eight in the morning. *She'd* been the one to pull him from his room each morning and shove whatever herbal concoction he insisted upon for breakfast down his throat. The likelihood of Horatio actually arising for a sunrise meditation after a night of cocktails was slim to none.

"As you can see if you look through the rest of the schedule, we've listed sunrise meditations for alternating mornings depending on the prior day's schedules. Due to the stressful nature of travel, we've kept tomorrow's sunrise meditation off the schedule to allow our guests to have a full night's sleep and an easy wake-up. As you've said yourself, sleep is the healthiest thing we can do for our chakra alignment." Paige smiled brightly at Horatio.

"I think our clients will expect a meditation," Horatio said, pushing his bottom lip out stubbornly.

"Certainly. There's no problem with you leading a meditation in the morning. We'll make sure the space is cleared for you. You're welcome to lead your meditations whenever you like."

"I..." Horatio's mouth worked as he realized she'd very neatly trapped him into leading the classes instead of having one of the staff do it. Now, he had nothing to complain about and he would have to be the one up at the butt crack of dawn.

"Isn't that great, baby? We can see the sun rise over the ocean and the waves crashing in the background will be perfect to center ourselves." Lily wrapped her arm through Horatio's.

"Right, of course. Be sure to let the others know that I'll be leading at least tomorrow's meditation."

"That sounds like a grand way to wake up," Whit said. He moved over and offered Horatio his hand. The men shook and did a weird little size-each-other-up thing where they looked each other up and down and pumped their hands a little too long. "I'm Whit, and one of the owners of Tranquila. You'll have a smashing time at the beach in the morning. It's such a lovely spot."

"Of course, I am sure it will be."

"And who is this gorgeous lady you have with you?" Whit's smile widened and Lily simpered at Horatio's side. Dropping his arm, she stepped forward like a bachelorette accepting a rose and extended her hand.

"I'm Lily, and I help run Yoga Soulone's studio." Lily quickly darted a smug look at Paige. Ah, her replacement then, Paige thought and almost laughed out loud. Lily could barely remember to get to class on time, let alone manage a studio.

"That sounds like an interesting job. You'll have to tell me all about it," Whit said, and drew Lily's hand to his lips for a kiss. Lily actually blushed and did a funny little curtsy motion, while Horatio's face flushed red.

Paige hadn't even thought about what would happen when Horatio and Whit's massive egos were pitted against each other, and now she reached back blindly for her drink.

And here she thought everything was running smoothly…

CHAPTER SIXTEEN

Mariposa had been correct. Paige didn't see a single guest again until they all staggered back in for the welcome reception that evening. Paige had taken the time that afternoon to review her schedule, as well as touch base with the other staff such as housekeeping. Feeling confident that everything was in order, all Paige could do was take a few deep breaths and wait for Horatio's next hissy fit. Which, knowing him, would be delivered whenever he next had an audience.

"Seltzer with lime?" Mariposa asked. For once, CeCe and Whit were not at the bar, and Paige briefly wondered if they'd decided to abstain for the night. "I'll put it in a tumbler so it looks like a gin and tonic."

"Perfect. I think it's best to keep my head about me with this group."

"You're going to have a problem with Horatio and Whit."

Surprised that Mariposa had picked up on that, Paige raised an eyebrow at her.

"You know Whit better than I do. Why do you say that?"

"Two Alpha dogs in the same room. It never goes well."

"I mean...would you really call either of these men Alphas?" Paige squinched up her nose as she thought about it, and Mariposa chuckled.

"Not by my terms. But by theirs, that's for sure."

Paige's eyes were drawn to where Jack had walked into the reception hall, his easy stride full of confidence, his muscles rippling under the Hawaiian-style shirt he'd put on for the occasion. If anyone was an Alpha...it was him.

"I'm wondering what I ever saw in Horatio."

"I was going to bring that up to you..." Mariposa smiled, her eyes also tracking Jack's movements. "But I didn't want to insult you."

"Can he be, like, my freebie? I mean, we all make mistakes in our dating lives, right?" Paige groused, propping her chin on her hand on the bar.

"My mistake cost me my freedom. But also gave me my biggest gift."

"Your daughter?"

"Yes. I'm tied to this island now, because she needs our extended family. And I wouldn't go back. I love my daughter even though my life is hard. It's worth it whenever I see her smile."

It was the most Mariposa had shared with her, and Paige warmed to the bartender. It seemed that now the guests had arrived there was a subtle shift in the us versus them mentality. Paige was part of the team now.

"I hope to meet her someday."

"She'll talk your ear off. Never stops. But she'll ask you a million questions about the States. It's a dream of hers to go one day."

"I hope you get to go. It's funny though – everyone from the States wants to come to places like this. I suppose we always want what's unfamiliar to us."

"Head's up." Mariposa nodded to the reception hall. Paige turned to see the guests had started to stream in with the bar in their sights. Paige straightened, slipped from the bar stool, and smiled as the guests approached. CeCe and Whit materialized as if by magic, having changed into evening cocktail attire, and both with wide smiles on their faces. CeCe reached for her martini and Paige blinked. How had Mariposa even concocted CeCe's drink that fast?

"Darlings!" CeCe waved to the group, "Please…join us for the happiest hour of the day. Well, every hour is happy at Tranquila Inn, isn't it? I trust you've all recovered from your travel?" CeCe gave a little shiver, like travel was for the commoners. "You'll want to refresh yourselves with some of our rum punch, I'm sure? If not, the lovely Mariposa will be happy to make you something else."

The lovely Mariposa barely hid her eye roll before she bent her head and began to fill the tiki mugs full of rum punch. It made sense, Paige realized, to create an easy batch order of drinks when there was one bartender and thirty or more guests. The men immediately converged around CeCe and Mariposa while Whit had drawn Lily, Nadia, and a few of the other women into what seemed to be a deep conversation on what was the best textile to use for yoga mats. Oh, he was good, Paige decided.

"Paige."

"Hello, Horatio. Did you find the accommodations to your taste?" Paige turned to where Horatio stood, dressed in another weird shirt tunic and loose flowing white pants. She wondered if the tunics were a new thing and based on the fact that Nadia was wearing a similar tunic, albeit without pants, Paige could surmise where the influence had come from.

"Yes, they are fine. I think you need to make it clear that *we* are running this retreat," Horatio said, his eyes narrowing as he shot a disgusted look at the group of women hovering around Whit. "Isn't it your job to make sure that everyone understands who is in charge?"

"I'm sorry…by *we* did you mean…?" Paige tilted her head up at Horatio in question.

"You and I, of course."

"As was outlined in the brochure that Yoga Soulone received…Tranquila Inn has packaged the retreat and put together the structure and schedule, while Yoga Soulone provides the teachers for the classes." The brochure that you refused to look at, Paige silently added. The only thing Horatio had actually cared about was the fact that his portion of the trip would be complimentary if he was able to fulfill a certain number of paid guest slots.

"Right, fine. So that means you and I are running this. Just like old times." Horatio gave her a heavy-lidded look and Paige was startled to realize that he was…hitting on her? Did he not recall what had *just* happened between them?

"Is it just like old times?" Paige asked lightly. "Because this feels different to me somehow. Hmm."

Paige tapped her finger against her mouth. "Let's see. Oh, that's right. I'm in charge here and you'll just be teaching the classes I've assigned to you. Actually, perhaps you are right. I did everything at Yoga Soulone, too, while you only taught. How's business running since I left?"

Horatio's face darkened, and Paige forced herself to take a deep breath. She really needed to check her impulse to mouth off to him because she'd promised Jack that she would keep Horatio happy on this trip. They weren't even that far into day one, and she was already poking the bear.

"And who is this handsome gentleman?" CeCe breezed up and hooked her arm through Horatio's, smiling up at him as though he was the second coming of Jesus. Horatio immediately bloomed under her smile.

"I'm Horatio. The owner of Yoga Soulone."

"That makes sense. I could just tell you had that aura of power about you. Not all men have that, you know. It's just this essence…do you understand what I mean? Oh…" CeCe looked around. "Where's your cocktail? Here, let's get you one." CeCe artfully pulled Horatio to the end of the bar to discuss his essence in more depth.

Well, now. She's a damn master, Paige thought with more than a hint of awe. Jack had been right when he'd said that CeCe and Whit would be a hit with the guests.

Four hours later and Paige was checking the time, wondering when the guests planned to get to bed. Particularly Horatio as he had his sunrise meditation to lead in the morning. Instead, the party had devolved from a simple welcome reception with a tasty dinner to a full-on dance party. Someone had cranked the music up, and now CeCe was swaying arm-in-arm with a couple, while Whit…

Paige looked around. Whit had disappeared, and so had Lily. Her heart dropped to her stomach as she realized what a catastrophic nightmare this could be if Horatio realized that Lily was canoodling with Whit and had a meltdown. Not to mention what CeCe was capable of pulling off, but considering she was rocking gently back and forth in the arms of a couple who seemed equally as enthralled…make that schnockered…as she was, Paige pushed that particular worry aside – her brain could only handle so much. She retreated to the bar to take stock for a moment where she found the men of the group all trying to one-up each other with their stories for Mariposa.

"And then…this guy tried to rob the convenience store. When I was right there. Can you even believe it?" Stan, who was five foot nine and rail thin, looked disgruntled as though this wayward criminal should have taken one look at him and run for the door.

"I'm shocked," Mariposa said, sliding his tip across the bar and into her tip jar. "He should've known better when he saw you."

"That's what I'm saying!" Stan slapped the bar with his open palm.

"Did I tell you about the time I broke up a bar fight with a biker gang?" Hal, another guest who was only marginally more well-built than Stan, leaned across the bar.

"Oh, wow! That must have been soooooo scary," Mariposa purred as she slid him another drink and accepted his tip.

"Nah, you just gotta know what to do. You gotta go low." Hal crouched like he was a defensive lineman.

"Are you sure about that? Isn't that just giving them access to smashing a beer bottle down on your head?" Stan asked and the two men began to argue the logistics of breaking up a bar fight. Mariposa smiled and, catching Paige's eye, she moved away from the men to the far corner of the bar where Paige stood and surveyed the situation.

"You're good at that," Paige observed.

"Just a little ego stroking. Everyone loves it – men and women alike. That dress really brings out your eyes." Mariposa nodded to Paige's dress.

"Oh, you think? Thanks…" Paige stopped before she preened for Mariposa. "Okay, point taken."

"No harm in complimenting people, hun. It makes them feel good and nobody gives me trouble."

"Speaking of trouble…" Paige leaned closer and lowered her voice, "I think Whit's disappeared with a guest. I'm not sure what to do."

"You don't do anything." Mariposa's dark eyes flitted to Paige's and held for a long look. "You hear me? You do nothing."

"But…what if CeCe flips out?"

"She won't. She only will if *you* call attention to it. You do nothing. If you don't listen to anything else I ever say to you…listen to this. Do. Not. Say. Anything. Understand?"

"But…" Paige looked back at the dance party. "What if…"

"This is not your hill to die on. *You* don't fight this battle. This is not your problem. None of your business. I'm not sure of any other way to say it to you."

"And if a guest gets mad?"

"That's not *your* problem. Your only problem is going to be making sure that Horatio doesn't have a fit because he looks like he's on the verge of a man-sized tantrum. That's the one you gotta be dealing with. Do not go to CeCe. Never go to CeCe with this."

"I get it…I just…" Paige realized it just felt shitty to cover up someone's cheating. Particularly when she'd just been on the receiving end of such treatment.

"They have…" Mariposa glanced back as one of the men called to her. "There's an understanding. CeCe and Whit are not your problem. Your man Horatio is the problem you gotta handle. Got it?"

"Loud and clear." It might not sit well with Paige, but Mariposa seemed to have an excellent read on things. And the woman wasn't wrong – was this the hill Paige wanted to die on? It was almost midnight and all of the guests were three sheets to the wind. The only thing she'd manage to do at this point would be to create a mess. Sighing, she glanced back at Mariposa before picking up the drink the bartender had slid to her. Mariposa met her look and then slid a finger across her throat in a cutting motion.

"I got it," Paige mouthed, widening her eyes and throwing a hand in the air. *Cool it with the threats, lady.*

Turning, her mouth fell open as she saw Horatio had taken his shirt off and was in a handstand with a circle of women around him. Some of the women shot glances at their partners who were currently fawning all over Mariposa. The women escalated their volume, likely hoping to catch the attention of the men, but all it did was serve to add fuel to Horatio's antics. Striding across the reception hall, intending to stop Horatio before he slipped and busted his head open, Paige drew up short when Jack stepped in front of her.

"Not so fast, hermosa," Jack said, a pleasant smile on his face though his eyes were serious.

"He's being ridiculous. I saw at least three people spill their drinks tonight. He'll slip and crack his head open."

"Then that's his prerogative."

"You can't mean that. It's…just look at him! He's trying to get all the attention in the room."

"So? Let him."

"But…" Paige looked around to where the party had split into small groups. There were a few men still making eyes at Mariposa, another group partied with CeCe in the middle of the hall, and the last group of women all surrounded Horatio. "He's being an ass."

"That he might be. But he's no longer your ass, is he?"

"Thank god for that," Paige muttered and took a slug of her drink before choking. Mariposa had made her a real gin and tonic this time and Paige was not expecting it. Jack slapped her lightly on the back as she coughed.

"You might want to slow down on those as well."

"Oh hush, I've been drinking seltzer all night. That's why I choked," Paige said, wiping tears from her eyes. "Mariposa gave me a real drink this time."

"Ah. Well, go slowly. I'll stay up until the last person gets to bed. For the safety of the guests and all that. We also have a night watchman on duty."

"That's smart. I suspect a lot of people will need help to their cottages. I don't even know what to say…these are not the people I know from back in California." Paige was having a hard time reconciling the wellness-obsessed guests that arrived fresh-faced to the yoga studio with this intoxicated group in front of her.

"Happens every time." Jack smiled. "I told you. People say they want to come here for a 'detox experience' but as soon as someone offers up some rum punch, it's game over."

"So…should I throw the schedule out the window?" Paige wondered. "Like is it just going to be a party for three weeks?"

"Nah, they'll still go to classes and stuff. But I don't think it will be as strict as you were thinking. I'd build in some flexibility with your time schedule."

"Horatio's leading a sunrise meditation tomorrow." Paige slapped a hand over her mouth when a giggle escaped. "He got in my face about it earlier."

"Did he now? And why is that?"

"Because I hadn't put it on the schedule. He made sure to confront me in front of others, too. I told him he was welcome to lead the meditation, so I think he's a bit cornered now."

"Perfect." With that, Jack walked to the group and Paige's mouth dropped open as his words carried back to her.

"Well done on the handstand, buddy! Will you be teaching everyone how to do that at your sunrise class tomorrow or have you called that off?"

Paige choked on a laugh as Horatio shot Jack a look of sheer loathing before schooling his face into a serene expression when the entire group of women shrieked with delight and then began to swarm Horatio to ask questions about the morning meditation.

When Jack caught her eye across the room, Paige gave him a thumbs-up and retreated to the kitchen to look for a snack.

She laughed the whole way there.

CHAPTER SEVENTEEN

Paige was not surprised when only a few stragglers joined the morning yoga session the next day. Word from the teacher of the morning classes was that Horatio had decided at the last minute to change his sunrise meditation to a sunset meditation, claiming the energy was stronger when the stars were out. Paige had smirked at that, but kept her comments to herself. She didn't know this new yoga instructor who had been saddled with the morning group, but Paige felt for her. She was young, green, and eager to please. Paige could see this woman easily being the next partner in Horatio's rotating bedroom door. She was even more surprised that Horatio was allowing others to teach classes.

Not my problem, Paige reminded herself, and gone to the kitchen to make sure everything was set for the day's lunch.

"Perhaps some comfort food?" Paige leaned against the counter and smiled at Martin. "I think our guests will be hungover."

"No problem, my lovely lady. I've got french fries, bacon, roasted potatoes, and lots of good brunchy stuff like pancakes."

"Perfect. I don't see a lot of this group green juicing after last night," Paige laughed. "Is it always like this?"

"It depends on the group. But at least for the first few days, people really cut loose. I don't think most guests even know how stressed they are until they get here."

"Yoga should relieve that stress."

"So does dancing naked on the beach and making out with random people."

"To each their own," Paige laughed again and took a spear of fruit with strawberries, pineapple, and mango chunks.

"You might try it someday. A little naked tango under the moonlight might do you some good."

"Not with this group." Paige sighed and pushed away from the counter. "I've already danced that dance, remember?"

"Find a different dance partner." Martin shrugged as if it was the easiest thing in the world.

"I think I'll dance by myself for a bit, thank you very much."

"Ah, relax. Take it poco poco. You'll hear the music one of these days."

"I didn't know you were so romantic, Martin."

"Don't you know? Chefs spend a lot of time thinking. They're on their feet all day…making love with their food. You ever need advice? Go to a chef."

"Some of the chefs I've worked with are downright scary." Paige thought back to a French restaurant she'd been a hostess at in college. If she didn't tiptoe around the chef and whisper in the kitchen, he'd explode.

"Those are chefs that are trying to make a statement with their food. I say let the food make the statement. You can make it as pretty as you want, but if it doesn't taste delicious…why bother?" Martin sniffed and turned with a spatula in his hand. "Who wants one of those poofs of foamed bubbles that is pretending to be a sauce? If you cook a steak, put a nice thick and creamy sauce next to it. Or none at all. But simple and delicious food is an art itself. No need for explosions and temper tantrums. Just pour some love into it."

"Pour some love into it. Got it."

"That's the ticket. Now, I like this song, and I'm going to dance while I cook. If you don't want to tango with me…get out of my kitchen."

Paige laughed as Martin winked at her. His flirting was harmless, as he was easily twenty years older than her and married, and she felt at ease with him. In fact, Luis and Martin were turning into two of her favorite people at Tranquila Inn. Her eyes found Jack, shirtless and drilling something into a wall across the reception room.

She'd dreamt of him last night. It came back to her, suddenly and with a punch to her gut, as his tanned muscles gleamed in the sunlight. It had been a decidedly naughty dream, one where she had *definitely* danced the dance, and it had left her aching for more. Sighing, Paige shook her head and forced the images out of her mind. It was only a dream and Jack certainly wasn't available to her. If she was to mature and grow, then one of those little life lessons should be: Don't sleep with your boss.

Even if her boss was incredibly delicious looking.

"Paige! There you are." Paige turned and stifled a sigh as Horatio strode across the reception lounge to her. His spray tan was starting to wane a bit, and he looked thin and sallow next to Jack's virility. "I've been looking for you."

"Good afternoon, Horatio. Martin is just finishing up on the late lunch as we moved the time a bit due to the guests enjoying a relaxing morning in their cabins. I trust you slept well? How was your sunrise meditation?"

"I moved it to sunset. As I've told you time and time again, sunset meditations are more powerful." Horatio shook his head as though he were scolding a child. "We'll need to have dinner set for after the meditation this evening."

"Of course. Will everyone be attending the sunset meditation and yoga session or should I plan food for any that would like to eat earlier?"

"Of course everyone will be attending. That is what we are here for. I trust you'll set up the space to be most advantageous for our uses."

"Naturally. We have a lovely space by the beach where you'll have uninterrupted views of the sunset. I do suggest you light the tiki torches as they have citronella to help keep the bugs away."

"Citronella?" Horatio sounded as if she'd said "heroin."

"Well, the bugs come out at sunset. Mosquitos. Sand flies. You'll want to take precautions, of course. They can get particularly bothersome."

"I certainly don't need nasty citronella smoke wafting over my followers as we commune with nature."

Paige raised her eyebrows at that. Since when had Horatio started referring to his clients as his followers? "Of course, I was only thinking of your comfort."

"Comfort is an illusion. Discomfort is where growth happens."

"Right, of course. In that case, I'll be sure to instruct Luis not to light the torches. Is there anything else you'll be needing for that time?"

"I'll expect you to keep the area clear."

"Yes, Horatio. I already said it would be set up for you."

"I meant of any stragglers who might interrupt the meditation."

"What stragglers? You're the only guests at the resort and this is a private beach."

"Meditation is for my followers only. Understood?" Paige followed Horatio's eyes to where Whit had materialized by the bar. Was Horatio honestly threatened by Whit? Paige would think it would be Jack that would cause Horatio discomfort, not Whit. Shrugging and wanting to be out of this conversation, Paige nodded again and held up her clipboard.

"Got it, Horatio. I've made notes. Guests only, no torches or bug repellants. Area cleared. I've got a meeting in a few minutes, so I have to run. Enjoy your lunch – I'm certain everything will be to your taste." Without waiting for an answer, Paige left Horatio behind and greeted every guest with a wide smile as she made her way across the reception hall, past the bar, and ducked into her office. Letting out a deep breath, Paige plopped into the seat behind her desk and took a moment. It was going to be a long three weeks with Horatio treating her like she was still his employee and her having to come to terms with the fact that she'd been blinded by him for so long. It was rewarding to know that she could look at him in a new light and see him for what he was, but it was hard not to beat herself up for falling under his spell for two years. If anything, she was feeling embarrassed for being a fool.

"Horatio got you down?"

Paige glanced up to her doorway where Jack leaned against the doorjamb and crossed his arms over his bare chest. A flash of the dream came back to her, one where they'd been tangled together, and she schooled her expression into a polite smile.

"A bit, I suppose."

"Missing him?" A look of surprise crossed Jack's face.

"Not even the slightest. I'm...well..." Paige laughed halfheartedly and put a hand to her face. "I'm embarrassed, actually. I can't believe I was into him for so long."

"Ah," Jack said, nodding. "I think we've all dated people that we aren't proud of."

"Yeah, but for two years? And I ran his business for him. It was all..." Paige made a circular motion with her hand. "Lumped together in one, I guess."

"It sounds like you didn't really have a lot of time to examine the relationship then, did you?"

"I guess not. I didn't think much of it, to be honest. It was sort of all consuming. Horatio and Yoga Soulone were my life because there were no boundaries between business and personal. It just...was."

"And when was the last time you took a vacation or stepped away from it?"

Startled, Paige looked at Jack. "Um, never really. Aside from retreats with Yoga Soulone's group, that is. And I was running around coordinating everything most of the time for those."

"Sounds to me like you haven't had a break in a long time. And if you had? Perhaps you would have had time to examine things more closely."

"Perhaps." Paige pursed her lips as she thought about it. Life with Horatio truly *had* been all-consuming.

"So? Don't be so hard on yourself. Live and learn, baby." Jack flashed her a grin.

"Definitely learning."

"Is he giving you a hard time?"

"Nope. Just treating me like I still work for him. Which, I guess I technically do since my job here is to make sure he's happy. And…" Paige held up a hand when Jack went to speak. "I'm totally fine with that. I'm just doing a little self-analysis along the way, I guess."

"Nothing wrong with some self-reflection every once in a while. Hey…I didn't see him at his sunrise meditation this morning." Paige knew Jack was up early every day.

"He's moved it to sunset. And get this – insisted on no bug spray or torches."

"Ooof." Jack rubbed a hand across his chest. "That's gonna hurt."

"I warned him. Trust me, I tried."

"Some people just like to learn the hard way."

Sure enough, Horatio insisted on doing it his way. Paige had intercepted him once more later in the afternoon to bring up the bug issue again, but Horatio dismissed her.

Considering her duty done, all Paige could do was wait for the aftermath.

"Why in the world would anyone go down to the beach at sunset when they could be at the bar?" CeCe, sensuous in a slinky coral-colored wrap dress and a chunky turquoise necklace, shuddered delicately as she gestured with her martini. "Don't they know about the bugs on the beach?"

"I warned them." Paige sighed. In the reception hall, they combatted the bug situation by lighting citronella torches at night and turning all the bamboo ceiling fans on for constant air movement. At discrete points around the hall, bottles of bug spray were also provided. While living in the tropics often seemed like a fantasy, there were certainly a few things that could make the reality more comfortable for people. Bug spray was one of those things.

"Maybe I'll go sit on the other side of the reception hall to watch the show."

"I think we all should," Mariposa said with a grin and that is how Paige found herself huddled with Whit, CeCe, and Mariposa peering through the branches of a plumeria tree like spies.

"And there it is," CeCe declared.

Sure enough, as the sun had begun to set, Paige could see a few people shifting in their positions, others surreptitiously swatting at their legs. In a matter of moments, it went from the first few people discreetly brushing their arms to the entire group outright swatting in the air. Horatio stood, raising his hands and clearly admonishing his "followers" to ignore the bugs and focus on his words. Paige bit her lip.

It only took one person to jump up, waving their hands in the air, before the rest of the group shifted. Like a mass exodus, one after the other, the guests streaked from the beach, swatting the air around them. Only Horatio, Lily, and Nadia remained.

"I give them thirty more seconds." Mariposa said.

"Bet you a dollar it's a minute," Paige said.

"Deal."

Neither won as the three lasted another minute and thirty-three seconds before Lily lost her nerve and bolted, with Nadia and Horatio following quickly. Paige followed Mariposa back to the bar, where the guests were liberally applying bug spray. Biting back her laughter, Paige greeted everyone.

"Who is ready for a rum punch?"

The entire group raised their hands.

CHAPTER EIGHTEEN

A few somewhat excruciating days later, Paige had settled into a rhythm. She started her morning by listening to any demands or complaints that Horatio had, stroked his ego, and then went about her day. Once she'd worked on removing her embarrassment over her history with Horatio, Paige had started to view him like any other demanding customer. Admittedly, he was overly familiar with her, but otherwise, Paige was beginning to feel hopeful that the next couple weeks should fly smoothly by. True to Martin's words, the first couple nights the guests had let loose but now were starting to settle into a more relaxed routine. All in all, Paige felt like the guests were happy and her employers seemed content, so for now she'd consider this retreat a win.

As though the universe had heard her thoughts, a bloodcurdling scream came from outside. Paige jumped up from her desk and flew to the door to see Jack racing across the sand. Paige followed suit, along with several guests, to see what had happened.

"It's Horatio! Oh, someone help him!" Lily screeched at the water line.

Paige skidded to a stop on the beach and shaded her eyes with her hand. Squinting, she could see Horatio, hands waving wildly in the air, far out in the water.

"Shark! Help! Shark! I'm bleeding!"

Shocked gasps emanated from the group that had gathered by the water.

"Somebody *do* something," Nadia wailed.

"Someone is. See?" Paige said, pointing to where Jack was already swimming to Horatio with a life ring hooked under his arm. Her heart raced as her eyes scanned the water looking for any fins poking up. Paige didn't want to think too deeply about the fact that she was more concerned for Jack than she was for Horatio.

A snort of laughter had her turning.

"How can you laugh?" Lily demanded to Whit, the one responsible for the laughter.

"Come now, dear heart. He's clearly fooling you."

"How can you say that?" Nadia hissed, glaring at Whit while Lily just looked confused.

"Because the reef line creates a barrier. The sharks can't swim over it. It's part of why our beach is so protected. Come, look." Whit beckoned them closer and Paige raised an eyebrow when Lily wrapped an arm around his waist. Horatio would *not* be happy when he saw that. "Now, look at where the water is a nice turquoise blue. See? That means there is just sand beneath it. See how there are no dark spots?"

The group gathered at the beach all followed to where he was pointing.

"Yes, I see," Lily said.

"Now, look out further. See that line of dark? And see where in some spots the rocks actually come out of the water? That's an entire line of reef that has grown so high that it reaches the top of the water and in some spots... through the surface."

"Oh," Lily said, still sounding confused.

"Which means that if a shark even could get over the top of the reef, it would have to be a very, very, very small one. Understand, darling? It's highly unlikely that Horatio will come to any harm right now."

"Oh, phew. I was worried." Lily looked adoringly up at Whit. He wrapped an arm around her shoulders and squeezed her closer.

"Not a thing to worry about other than the possibility that he will drown from his own panic attack."

"Jack's there. He'll handle it," Nadia said, a note of admiration in her voice as Jack reached Horatio. Uh-oh, Paige thought, and made a mental note to try and keep those two focused on Horatio or she'd have the mother of all temper-tantrums on her hands in the form of one insecure Horatio.

Out in the water, it looked like Horatio was arguing with Jack, before Jack managed to cut him off entirely by hauling him onto the life ring and dragging him back through the water. It didn't look easy, Paige thought, but she noticed how neatly Jack managed to slice through the water, with strong kicks bringing them quickly to shore. When they reached a point where their feet could touch, Jack stood and dragged Horatio a few more feet before stopping and looking patiently down at the yoga instructor.

Nadia was the first to break the silence.

"Oh, Horatio! Are you okay?" She dashed into the water and bent over him. Paige pressed her lips together as Horatio struggled to get off the life ring and ended up rolling over to splat face-first in the water. When he stood, looking like a wet chicken, his expression was indignant. "You poor thing."

"I'm bleeding." Horatio walked from the water and pointed to where a long scrape bled lightly on his foot. "Sharks were closing in on me."

"Were they?" Jack asked, lifting his chin in mock surprise.

"They were! I saw two of them! Big ones, too. They smelled the blood, I'm sure of it." Horatio insisted. His eyebrows went up when more than one person laughed. "How can you laugh? I almost died! They were there. They were coming for me!"

"But…" Lily said, looking up at Whit. Paige noticed she hadn't dropped her arms from around him.

"How did you get cut, Horatio?" Paige smoothly inter-cepted Lily's explanation. The group around them had grown and more than one person was now outright laughing at Horatio. The man's face had grown deep red, and Paige knew a temper tantrum was on its way.

"I accidently kicked a rock. I was so focused on the beautiful coral and communing with Mother Ocean that I must not have seen it. It really hurts. I must be cut very deeply." Horatio pushed his bottom lip out.

"You probably kicked the coral," Jack said, hoisting the life ring around his arm, "which is why it stings so much. Likely a very shallow scrape, but the coral has its own protective mechanism, which is why it stings for you. It's a living animal, after all, and you shouldn't kick it."

Oh man, Paige thought, as Horatio's expression grew mutinous and the rest of the group shook their heads in admonishment. *This is not gonna be good.*

"Excuse me, but you have no idea what I did or did not kick. I told you it was a rock, didn't I? And clearly the sharks smelled my blood which is why they were circling. I'm lucky I didn't lose my foot!" Horatio stomped the offending foot into the sand. Paige had to wonder how much it really hurt if he was stomping with it.

"Sure, buddy. It was a rock then. I didn't see any sharks though," Jack said, an easy smile on his face like he was trying to placate a toddler. "Likely just a bit of panic kicking in for you. It's nothing to be ashamed of though. You are out of your element and you got hurt. That can kick up your adrenaline pretty easily and throw you into a panic."

"I was not panicking." Horatio held a hand to his chest. "I was calm. I was merely worried about the sharks with my blood in the water. That's a normal thing to be worried about."

"Except there were no sharks," Jack continued. "But you're not wrong – sharks can certainly smell blood. However, this was all just a combination of you getting hurt and a simple panic response. It's okay now. Everything's going to be just fine." With that, Jack patted Horatio on the arm, and then moved through the crowd that opened up to make way for him. He shot Paige a wink as he went past, and she could only shake her head slightly. She wanted to laugh, god she wanted to laugh so hard, but knew she was going to have to put her big girl pants on and baby Horatio's ego for a while. At least Whit had disappeared, Paige realized. That was one less problem she'd have to navigate.

"I did not panic." Horatio sniffed and looked around at the rest of the group standing on the beach. "There was blood in the water."

"But Whit said sharks can't get in here." Lily, in a scrap of a bikini, put her hands on her hips as she looked up at Horatio. "And Whit says you probably did hit coral. It stings, you know."

"Oh, Whit says, does he?" Horatio strode across the sand, casting a disgusted look at Lily. "What does Whit even know? The man doesn't do yoga, and I've never once seen him swim in the water. He's certainly no expert."

"But…he's the owner. Don't you think he knows the water here?" Lily asked, tagging along automatically after Horatio.

"Whit doesn't know shit, Lily. I'm the one who was out there. I know what I was facing!"

"Yeah, Lily. We're just lucky Horatio is alive, aren't we?" Nadia said, running after Horatio and hooking her arm through his.

"Of course." Lily schooled her expression. "We were very worried for you. It must have been so scary to be out there on your own like that."

"I wasn't scared," Horatio scoffed and tossed his hair over his shoulder. "But you have to take blood in the water seriously. The sharks, you know, they can smell it for miles. It's a big deal."

His voice trailed off as they walked out of sight, and

Paige turned to the rest of the group, a professional smile on her face.

"They only get nurse sharks here," Hal said. "I looked it up before I came. Well, at least in near shore. And those sharks are like big puppies. You guys don't have to worry if you go in the water. In fact, having the reef like it is probably means the snorkeling is actually really good."

"Do you think so?" Another woman asked.

"Well, I'm a diver and I typically jump in the water when I see sharks." Hal laughed. "But Jack wasn't wrong. It was more likely that Horatio just scared himself and set off a panic reaction. Frankly, he's lucky he didn't drown, what with all the flailing about he did."

"He's obviously not confident in the water," another woman said.

"We offer snorkel gear if anyone else would like to give it a go. It sounds like Hal is pretty familiar with coral reefs. Maybe he'd be willing to take a few of you out if you'd like to explore?" Paige spoke, wanting to divert the group from talking much more about Horatio. She didn't care if they dethroned him after this trip, but she wasn't ready to deal with his fall from grace *during* the retreat.

"I think I would like to. If there really aren't any sharks?"

"Even if there are, they're really cool. I promise. You'll be fine."

Soon, Hal had an interested group of snorkelers hanging on his every word, and Paige left them to return to the reception hall to deal with whatever fire needed to be put out next. There, she found Whit and CeCe at their permanent spots by the bar and Jack nowhere to be seen.

"Sharks." CeCe sniffed, taking a sip of her martini. "There haven't been sharks here for years. Except for that one that got stuck after the big swells from that one storm. Remember that, darling?"

"I certainly do, my sweet. It was a group effort to get him back out over the reef. Right tricky, it was." Whit beamed down at his wife and they began to reminisce.

"How long have you lived here?" Paige asked, accepting her glass of soda water and lime from Mariposa. The bartender knew now to only give Paige a drink if she specifically requested it. Paige had promised herself once this group was gone, she was going to get good and shit-faced. But until then? She was going to keep her wits about her.

"Oh, a few years now, right?" CeCe squinted at Whit in question.

"Probably that. Maybe a few more. It all blends together, doesn't it now?" Whit laughed and shrugged. "Long enough, I suppose."

"Oh, you think? Has the time come?" CeCe twinkled up at Whit.

"For another project? Maybe. We've got so many projects here still, darling."

"Oh, we do at that. We're just so busy."

Paige had come to realize they were constantly nattering on about all the projects they were doing, however she'd yet to see any physical evidence of these projects. It was beginning to become a bit of a running joke in her mind – two points every time she could spot a possible project. Or any evidence of CeCe or Whit actually working on said projects.

"Well, it's a nice spot. I think the guests are really happy here," Paige said as she wasn't really sure what CeCe and Whit were going on about.

"I would hope so. We certainly poured enough money into it, didn't we love?" CeCe's words sounded more like a criticism than a compliment as she looked at Whit. Paige eased back as the two began to argue in hushed tones.

"So Jack saved Horatio, huh?" Mariposa smiled a mile-wide grin at Paige. "What I wouldn't have given to see that."

"Oh, it was worth every hour of angst over that man. Jack dragged him in like a turtle flailing on its back."

"Oh my god. Tell me everything."

CHAPTER NINETEEN

The days drew out, falling into a pattern of yoga classes, a daily Horatio hand-holding session, and heightening tensions between several members of the group. Paige found it oddly like watching a soap opera from afar, except, she had a direct part in the outcome as the players often came to her to gripe about each other. A few of the top complaints: Whit disappearing on late-night beach walks with different women. The men all falling head over heels for Mariposa – even though many of them were there with their partners. Horatio not getting enough attention. Oddly enough, CeCe was never at the center of complaints – as both men and women alike warmed to her cheerful personality.

Except for one person, that is.

Paige had been on her way to her office to escape Horatio one day when she'd happened upon a whispered argument between Jack and CeCe. They'd dispersed when they'd seen her – Jack shooting her a glare before disappearing into the garden. CeCe had pasted a smile on her face and chattered at Paige about a project she was working on in their personal quarters – something about refacing a cabinet. The day CeCe refinished a cabinet was the day that Paige would see a shark walk on land.

She'd had a moment to overhear a bit of their argument before they'd cut it off at her approach. It had sounded like it was about CeCe's and Jack's past. There had been something about finances and money owed…but she hadn't been able to make it out. Paige hoped that Tranquila Inn wasn't in trouble. Because as weird as everyone was here, she was starting to find her own pace and thought she could end up enjoying this job. She'd yet to see anything else of the island, but one of these days she planned to explore more. The problem was – and this was something she always ran into – the balance between her work and her life was seriously skewed.

"Hey."

Paige looked up to see Jack at her office door.

"Hey."

"I'm heading into town for a supply run. Want to come with? It's been brought to my attention that you haven't left the hotel once since the last time you went to town." Jack smiled at her like he was asking her to skip school and go smoke dope in the parking lot.

"It would be nice to have a change of scenery. Do we really get to go play?"

"Boss says it's okay." Jack looked at his watch. "Meet me out front in fifteen?"

"That should work. I'll just go grab my purse and put my stuff away." Even though she still had a ton of paperwork, Paige found herself excited at the prospect of a little downtime. She'd taken to retreating to her office as much as she could lately. Managing Horatio was like trying to calm down a toddler that had been set loose in a candy store. It would be nice to be completely unavailable to him for an afternoon.

Paige changed into a flowy dress in soft blue with simple white beading stitched at the neckline. She'd taken to throwing her hair up in a loose bun on her head due to the heat and continued with her no-makeup theme. Grabbing her purse, she paused as she glanced in the mirror.

She looked relaxed, Paige realized. For the first time in ages, there was color in her cheeks and the tension lines in her forehead had smoothed out. Paige added some simple silver hoop earrings and grabbed her cell phone. She wanted to take pictures for Jane, who had been pestering her for updates on the whole Horatio situation. Paige had been too busy to give her much detail, but perhaps she'd get a chance to send some photos of the island to her friend today.

Humming, Paige locked her cottage and made her way to the reception hall where CeCe found her immediately.

"Hello, gorgeous. You look cheerful today. Are you off with Jack then?" CeCe fingered the long gold rope chain at her throat.

"I am." Paige tilted her head at CeCe in question. "Is that okay?"

"Perfectly alright. I can't imagine why you'd think I'd be bothered."

"If you need me for anything here, I'm happy to stay."

"Of course not, darling. I've got everything under control. I could run these retreats with my eyes closed."

"Of course." Then why had she hired Paige?

"Take as long as you need, darling. I must be off. I'm in the middle of a project." CeCe winked at her and headed for the bar. Paige wondered if her project was finishing the martini that Mariposa had left for her. Turning, she high-tailed it to the front drive and found Jack waiting in the battered Suzuki. Her breath skipped as she studied him unnoticed for a moment. He'd pulled a baseball hat on that had the Tranquila Inn logo on the front and mirrored glasses shaded his eyes. A dark blue t-shirt contrasted nicely with his tan, and he drummed his fingers against the doorframe to the beat of the music from the radio. When Jack saw her, he flashed her a wide grin, and a delicious little shiver went through Paige.

Do not sleep with the boss.

She shouldn't have to remind herself of that, Paige thought, as she climbed into the little SUV. Like…that should just go with the territory. Jack was off-limits. She was living out of a duffle bag in another country and had no solid life plan other than to get through this retreat. Hopefully, she would make a good impression on her employers and they would let her stay around long enough to figure out what her plan was. Which made it imperative that she kept her mind away from naughty daydreams and on her future instead.

"What's with the look? Do you not want to go to town?" Jack asked.

"Oh. No. I do. I was just having a moment of contemplation."

"It didn't look particularly fun. Might I suggest avoiding that in the future?"

Paige laughed and leaned back against the seat, looking out the window as the SUV trundled over the rough drive through the brush to get to the main road.

"It was my future I was contemplating though."

"From that look, you may just want to take your future day by day." Jack reached over and turned up the radio, drumming his fingers on the steering wheel, and Paige took the cue that he didn't want to talk. Which was fine. She didn't much feel like talking either. That was the one thing about customer service – she found herself talking *all* day long. Grateful for a reprieve, Paige let the music and the island breezes wash over her as they wound their way along the coast into town. It was one of those perfect island days – cloudless and breezy – and the sun turned the water a perfect shade of turquoise blue.

It wasn't a bad spot to hunker down, Paige mused, as Jack looked for parking in the little downtown. She was sure the island had its problems, as did she, but for once, Paige was going to take someone else's advice and try not to think too much about her future. She'd land on her feet, as she always did, no matter what the future held.

"We need cleaning supplies for our housekeeping department and a few kitchen staples for Martin. After that, I think we might be able to sneak in a cheeky beer if you'd like?"

"Can we go back to the same spot we were at before? I liked that bar."

"Yeah, no problem. Let's get through our errands quickly."

An hour later, they had acquired everything on their

list. Paige was sweaty once again, having helped haul the packages to the Suzuki.

"How do you know people aren't going to steal your stuff?" Paige wondered, looking dubiously at the mound of packages in the back of the little SUV. Jack hadn't bothered to lock the doors, nor had he rolled the windows up. Anyone walking by could reach in and grab the contents of the backseat.

"Most people know my car. And if they need to steal cleaning supplies or flour then they need it more than we do."

"That's a very trusting attitude," Paige said, falling in step next to Jack as they wound their way down a narrow side street and out to the harbor walk. "Don't you worry that people will take advantage of you? Especially if they think you can afford it?"

"I choose to believe in the good in people." Jack shrugged as they reached the little thatched-roof bar. "We're a small island. Word gets around if things get stolen."

"Interesting." Paige smiled at the bartender – a pretty older woman with thick creases in her face.

"A bucket of beers again?" Jack glanced at her.

"Sure."

Once the bartender had returned with the bucket full of mini-beers and Jack had opened one for her, Paige leaned back and let out a long breath. Sipping her beer, she nodded her head to the low pulse of music coming from a tiny radio behind the bar and watched people wander past on the waterfront.

"So you seem to be holding up alright," Jack said, gesturing with his beer.

"So do you," Paige said.

"Me? How so?" Jack laughed.

"With CeCe and Whit," Paige explained. There was a familiarity between the three of them that Paige just couldn't put her finger on. It went past the normal friendly employee/employer relationship. And the same with the way Jack always spoke with easy affection about Mariposa. There were so many undercurrents that Paige couldn't yet decipher the relationships of the staff at Tranquila Inn.

"Ah." Jack took a long pull of his drink and didn't say anything else.

"Why did they buy Tranquila Inn? Have they owned other hotels?" Paige prodded, realizing that Jack was not going to expand on his relationship with CeCe, though Paige desperately wanted to know what they had been arguing about so fiercely the other day.

"CeCe and Whit have a tendency to be…impulsive. They often throw themselves into projects as a manner of escape." Jack pressed his lips together in a thin line. "Tranquila was just their latest."

"Like…on to the next shiny bright thing?" Paige suggested.

"Exactly. CeCe's attention span isn't great and frankly, I'm surprised they've been here as long as they have." Jack's words spoke of a long-bred familiarity.

"How did you come to work for them? Like have you known them for a while?" Paige asked.

"Yes."

It was like pulling teeth with this one, Paige glowered at her beer. "What was Tranquila Inn before they bought it?"

"Blue Beach Resort. It was fairly run-down, to be honest. But CeCe had read an article about opening bed and breakfasts and somehow that translated into buying a run-down hotel on a tiny Caribbean island where tourism has suffered with recent hurricanes."

Sidetracked, Paige looked at him in surprise.

"Have there been many storms? The downtown looks to be in fairly good shape."

"It is. But if you go further south, you'll see many of the big hotels are still recovering from a storm a few years ago. In fact, it's what made Tranquila Inn such a steal of a purchase – and actually not the stupidest piece of real estate to buy. While the big hotels are still recovering, Tranquila was able to open at reduced rates while the renovations were happening. We've had a surprisingly steady business, though I'd like to see more return guests. It's hard to impress people when you're still painting the rooms and so on."

"It sounds like you've done a good job with everything. This retreat seems fairly successful. Well..." Paige trailed off and remembered Mariposa's words about Whit.

"But...?" Jack turned to study her.

"There's some tension, I'll admit. I think some people are questioning where Whit disappears to at night." Paige carefully kept her gaze on her beer bottle, worried she'd be setting off an explosion with Jack – particularly if he was fond of CeCe.

"That doesn't sound like a problem that falls under our domain."

"But…" Paige glanced up at him. "Isn't customer experience something we, well, *I*, handle?"

"This isn't a kid's camp, Paige." A note of warning threaded through Jack's tone.

"So you just want me to ignore what is happening?" Paige asked, pushing the topic. But seriously – he couldn't be blind to it, could he? CeCe was all but falling off tables dancing wasted with guests every night, while Whit disappeared with a different guest for "long walks" on the beach.

"Yeah, I do." Jack leveled a look at her. "These are adults. They are making their own choices. You can't control what they do. Understood?"

"I…" Paige trailed off and instead took a large gulp of her beer. "Understood." It went against everything in her nature not to try and smooth over the tensions that were clearly growing in the group.

"Poco poco," Jack said. "Let it flow. It's the island way."

"Right, it appears that I may struggle with that concept." Understatement of the year, Paige thought.

Jack's lips quirked before he took another pull from his beer bottle.

"Most do. You'll get it in time."

"How much time?" Paige demanded. "Because I'd like to feel that way now."

Jack laughed and leaned back in his stool. "Horatio bugging you?"

"Honestly, while he's annoying, it's nothing that I'm

not used to. I don't think I realized how much handholding I did for him. But now that I'm viewing it outside the relationship, I realize I was essentially his minder for the last couple years. I'll be happy when he goes home."

"Not missing the studio?"

"I mean…" Paige thought about it. "Not really. I miss some of the clients. But, I'm so busy here and I enjoy tackling the challenges that are presented each day. I think, more than anything, that is what I would miss. The pride that comes with managing a business, problem-solving, and the reward of happy customers. But if I can do the same here, then I think I'll be happy."

"You think you'll stay on?" Jack didn't look at her as he opened another beer. Paige's stomach did a little flip. Was this a performance review or was he asking for personal reasons?

"I…I'd like to. I'd like to get through a full season and see how things go. Admittedly, this first group is a little weird for me what with my personal history and all. But I am looking forward to working with the next retreats and seeing how each group differs in their needs and so on."

"I think you're an asset to the business. I know I'd like for you to stay."

"Thanks." Paige smiled shyly at Jack. Warmth bloomed inside her, and she realized it had been a long time since someone had complimented her on her work. Horatio was in the business of offering critiques and had rarely praised her. No wonder her chakras had been a mess. "Do you plan to stay on? It sounded like you enjoyed bouncing around the world."

"I'll admit…I do miss traveling. I'm hoping to get off-island in the low season. I usually prefer to come in and clean up problems and move on than to stay. But...this place feels different to me. Maybe I'll settle in for a while."

"No woman pining for you in Indonesia or some other far-off place?" Paige teased.

"Not that I'm aware of." Jack laughed and took a sip of his beer. "I've been too busy to date lately anyway."

"What's your type?" Paige asked. Maybe the beer was making her emboldened, she thought, and bit her lip, hoping she hadn't crossed a line.

"Physically or personality?" Jack laughed.

"Both?"

"Physically? Hmm...I like a woman shorter than me with some meat on her bones. None of this stick-thin nonsense. Mentally? Smart, funny, and independent. Likes yoga. Travels impulsively. Fights scorpions. I don't like women that are too needy or have to be coddled all the time."

Heat bloomed through Paige at his words.

"I don't blame you. It's exhausting to have to hand-hold. I know it." Paige managed to speak past the urge to kiss him.

"Not missing that, are you?" Jack laughed.

"Nope. I much prefer an independent man who can take care of things on his own." Paige laughed and glanced at Jack. For a moment, their gazes held until Jack broke the look.

"I think you'd be quite the catch, Paige."

CHAPTER TWENTY

R estless that evening, Paige turned in her bed as her thoughts once more drifted to Jack. The dreams she'd been having about him hadn't abated, and if she was going to be honest with herself in the dark of the night – she liked him. As in, *really* liked him. She wasn't sure if it was because he was such a study in contrasts to Horatio, the man who needed constant attending-to and whined incessantly, or if it was simply because he was a confident and sexy man who actively respected the decisions she made. It seemed to be such a silly thing, to have her choices acknowledged and agreed with, and yet it filled her with a sense of pride that she hadn't realized she'd been missing.

Could she...should she...make a move on Jack? The thought alone had her laughing out loud. This was the moment when a fairy godmother was supposed to show up and whack her on the head with a magick wand to stop her from being a complete idiot. Hadn't she repeatedly told herself that banging the boss was a no-no? No matter how enthusiastic Jane was on the topic of sweaty beach sex, Paige was certain it would land her right back where she started – with her duffle bag at the dusty airport.

No. It was best she kept her fantasies to herself. No matter how much she wanted a taste of Jack. It didn't help that the man walked around shirtless half the time and had bronzed skin like some Adonis. No, that really didn't help. Rolling over again, Paige pounded a fist into her pillow. What had he meant when he'd said that she was a great catch? He'd definitely been flirting, right? The questions zipped around her head, making her sigh with frustration, until she finally swung her legs off the bed and stood. Paige walked across the room and examined her air conditioner. Was this thing not working or was the thought of being with Jack driving her temperature up? She might as well be a cat parading through the yard yowling for a mate as heated as she was.

Making a quick decision, Paige slipped into her bikini and grabbed a towel. She left her cottage and padded quietly across the sand to where the ocean beckoned to her. Now that she knew that no sharks could get into the little bay in front of Tranquila Inn, Paige felt confident going into the water at night. Standing at the edge of the beach, she took a few deep breaths, working to center herself as the light of the moon danced a trail across the gentle waves. Stepping forward, Paige smiled as the water embraced her, drawing her close like a lover, cooling the fire that raced across her skin.

"Oh, this is heaven," Paige said out loud, kicking back to float in the salt water and look up at the stars.

"I see you're not the only one who needed a break."

"Shit!" Paige's head dropped under water at the shock of a voice near her head and then she shot up, water sputtering from her lips as she whirled around. "Jack!"

"Sorry, I didn't mean to startle you." Jack's grin flashed in the moonlight. "I was going to dive under and tug your leg down but didn't want to give you a heart attack. Plus, you look pretty strong."

"Smart move. I would have attacked." Paige brought a hand to where her heart hammered in her chest. "You really need to stop sneaking up on people."

"It's the middle of the night. What am I supposed to do? Wear a bell on a collar around my neck?"

Paige's mind strayed to thinking of Jack with a collar, kneeling before her.

"What's that smile for?" Jack demanded, and Paige realized she'd gotten lost in the naughty little image for a moment.

"Nothing. Sorry. Okay, I think I'm safe from a heart attack. Do you come down here every night?" Paige asked. She kicked up and floated in the water once more, enjoying the sensation of weightlessness in the buoyant salt water.

"Here and there. It depends on the night. Or when I can't sleep."

"Do you have problems sleeping, too?"

"Depends." Jack smiled when she rolled her eyes at him. "I'm guessing you do?"

"Depends," Paige mimicked and laughed when he splashed water toward her. "Only when something is bothering me."

"What's bothering you, Paige?" Jack asked, drawing closer.

You, Paige thought. Instead, she just shook her head.

"And here I thought we were friends."

"We are friends." Which is why I can't tell you that I want to ride you until I can't think straight, Paige added silently.

"So, what's bugging you?"

"You first," Paige said.

"Stubborn, are you?"

"I have my moments." Paige tore her gaze away from him, because she was certain if they continued this line of questioning she was about to break her "Do Not Bang the Boss" rule. Instead, she looked back up at the stars.

"Fine." Jack sighed and Paige was surprised to find he'd drifted even closer, so that his head was close to her. "It's you."

The words, but a whisper at her ear, sent heat flashing through her body.

"Did I...have I...done something wrong?" Paige asked, turning so she faced him. Only his head was visible above the dark water, and the moonlight gleamed against his eyes.

"No, that's not..." Jack half-laughed and looked away, seeming to argue with himself before turning back to her. "I find you...enchanting."

"Oh," Paige breathed as Jack floated even closer. His hand brushed against her arm and the sensation caused little ripples of lust to spike through her.

"A siren, really. Maybe you *are* a mermaid."

"From what you've said about mermaids, you'd better

be careful because it's likely I'm about to murder you then."

Jack threw his head back and laughed and when he turned back, his lips were on hers before Paige could take her next breath. The moment hung suspended as the press of his lips to hers shot heat straight to her core. Jack wound his arms around Paige, pulling her so that her legs wrapped around his waist. She was cocooned in his embrace as they floated, enthralled with each other. Pulling back, Paige gasped for air, and then she was lost once more as Jack found her lips again, nipping softly with his teeth, the taste of him salty on her tongue. Lust bloomed within her and it took everything in her power to break the kiss.

Paige swallowed as her eyes met Jack's, and their eyes locked in silence for a moment, the ocean cradling them. Rolling on to her back, she looked up at inky night sky and smiled when his hand found hers in the water. Together they floated, the tension of the kiss entwined between them, their little secret shared with the stars.

CHAPTER TWENTY-ONE

His kiss still warmed her days later. Maybe it was just in her mind, but Paige felt like something had shifted significantly with them. In the coming days, while there were no more stolen kisses no matter how much Paige hoped, Jack had started stopping by her office more frequently or seeking her out to solve one problem or the other. It felt nice that someone with his experience would defer to her opinions on how to handle the clientele, and Paige found herself humming as she went about her work each day.

"Do him," Jane exclaimed when Paige had finally found a moment to call her friend and catch her up. "Yes. Hot sweaty sex on the beach."

"That sounds buggy and gross. Don't you know that sand will get in every crevice?" Paige winced as she crossed her legs and thought about the abrasive nature of sand.

"So? That's what showers are for. Do him. *Please* do

him. I have to live vicariously through you." A child's shout sounded in the background.

"I don't think it is lack of sex that got you in your current position," Paige pointed out.

"Yeah, but that's married sex. Yours is vacation-like sex."

"There is no sex. Sex will not be happening."

"More's the pity. Live a little. I gotta run." A crash sounded and Paige was left staring at her phone.

"Why is sex not happening?"

Paige screeched and dropped the phone on her desk. She glanced up to where Jack stood in the door to her office and her face heated.

"Ignore that please. I was just trying to catch up with my friend Jane who, apparently, is sex-deprived due to her three children constantly being underfoot."

"Ah." Jack studied her for a moment, and Paige's cheeks heated even further. "Horatio is requesting your presence. Apparently he doesn't take orders well."

"This is not a newsflash. I'm coming, I'm coming." Anything to get away from this conversation, Paige thought. Jack didn't back up from the doorway, causing her to brush close to him as she passed. Her mind slid back to the increasingly naughty dreams she'd been having about him recently and she blushed once more. Damn Jane for putting those thoughts in her head.

"Everything okay?" Jack asked as she all but ran away from her office.

"Yup, all good," Paige called over her shoulder and hurried to the reception area. When she didn't spot Horatio, she continued on down to the beach where she found him with a group of his most devout yogis huddled around him.

"There you are." Horatio had finally gotten a real tan and wasn't looking too bad now that he'd ditched the weird tunics in favor of simple board-shorts. "I've been waiting for you."

"I didn't know you needed me today. This afternoon was meant to be free time for everyone as it is the end of another week heavy with classes." As we'd agreed upon when we reviewed the itinerary, Paige silently added.

"Jack is a problem," Horatio said, and Paige looked at him in confusion while the group of yogis all nodded silently around him.

"Excuse me? What's wrong with Jack?"

"He said we can't take out the SUPs." Tranquila Inn offered stand-up paddle boards for the guests to use.

"Why would he say that? That's odd."

"I showed him where I wanted to go. And he said no, because the tide is coming in."

"Where do you want to go?" Paige asked. "I don't see the problem if you go out front here because of the reef-break. This is a nice calm bay for you to be on the board in."

"I don't want to go here. The energy's off." Horatio sniffed and the group around him nodded again.

"Right. Okay." Paige pinched her nose, squinting at Horatio and wishing she'd grabbed her sunglasses. "Where is it you'd like to go?"

"There. See?" Horatio pointed to the dock where Tranquila Inn had their own private dinghy boat tied. Past the boat lay calm blue water and a little sand dune area. "I want to go to the sand bar. It's not far and the energy flows better there."

"Yeah, Paige. The energy is better on the sand bar." Nadia put her hand on her hip.

"I mean, don't you think it's best to trust Jack? He certainly knows the waters around here better than I do. If he says not to go, I'd listen."

"Do we have to listen to everything he says?" Nadia asked.

Paige reminded herself of Jack's own words to her – these were adults she was dealing with.

"I don't think you have to listen to everything he says, no. However, if it's a safety issue, I'd strongly advise you to listen to what Jack says here. He's in the business of making sure you are all happy and safe. I'd trust his judgement call on this one."

"So, she's not saying no then. Okay, everyone, let's head out."

"But…" Paige looked at Horatio in surprise. "I really don't think it's wise for you to do this, Horatio."

"What could possibly be the problem? Look how calm the water is. You're overreacting, Paige. Just like you always do."

Stung, Paige closed her mouth while Lily and Nadia snickered. A few of the group dropped back, clearly heeding her words, while a small group followed Horatio to where the SUPs were stacked on the beach. She should probably stop him, Paige thought, but a part of her hoped he'd float off to sea and she'd never have to deal with him again. Maybe that was one of those angry chakras Horatio had lectured her about…

Sighing, Paige retreated to the reception hall to grab her sunglasses and to locate Jack, as she was certain he had a good reason for not wanting Horatio to use the paddle boards.

"What's got you down, mama?" Luis asked from where he was trimming a bush.

"Horatio's an idiot and likely going to get himself killed."

"So let him." Luis shrugged one shoulder.

"I don't think that will be good for our hotel image. *Guest dies while paddle boarding unsupervised.*"

"Maybe not. But still his choice."

"Have you seen Jack?" Paige asked, working to tamp down on her exasperation.

"I think he was with CeCe last I saw him."

"And that would be where?"

"Where else?" Luis laughed.

"Right. At the bar. See ya." Paige took off in the direction of the bar and even from a distance she could see that CeCe and Jack were arguing. Mariposa was nowhere to be seen. Jack broke off as Paige drew close, spotting her over CeCe's shoulder. The older woman turned at his look, and for a moment, her expression took Paige's breath away.

A deep-rooted sadness etched the fine lines of her face, and her eyes were haunted by what ghosts Paige did not know. It was like looking at an entirely different person than the animated CeCe she knew. Upon seeing Paige, CeCe's expression cleared and was replaced with her usual jovial smile.

"Hello, gorgeous! Just delighted to see you. Join us,

will you?" CeCe gestured to the bar where her martini sat and a can of Coca-Cola was out for Jack.

"I can't right now. I need Jack, if you can spare him?"

"Of course. We weren't discussing anything important, were we?" CeCe's tone was steady as she turned back to Jack.

"That's one interpretation," Jack bit out before turning to Paige. His expression was mutinous, and Paige debated adding fuel to that particular fire.

"Um, Horatio's gone ahead with taking the paddle-boards out. I advised him against it, but..." Paige trailed off as Jack slammed his fist down on the bar.

"That fucking idiot! How many times do I have to tell him no? He's like a damn child. I thought I sent you out there to handle him." Jack strode off without another word and Paige gritted her teeth, staring after him.

"Don't mind his temper, darling. He's like all men – they never know how to appropriately deal with their feelings." With that, CeCe turned back to *her* preferred numbing mechanism – a martini.

"I'm just going to go make sure Jack doesn't murder Horatio."

"It wouldn't be much of a loss for the world, would it, darling?" CeCe threw her head back and laughed and Paige beelined back to the beach to stop a potential murder in progress. There she found Jack, standing on the dock, all but vibrating with anger. The rest of the retreat had caught wind of the drama and the guests now peppered the beach, looking to where Horatio had managed to get his little group to the sand bar.

They'd piled their paddles together on one side of the

sandbar and then haphazardly pulled their boards on top of each other. This left the group in the middle, dutifully following whatever Horatio was expounding on as he waved his arms in the air and turned in a wide circle. Paige sighed as they began a series of Sun Salutations, and knew that they would be there as long as Horatio demanded they be or until Jack went out in the boat and ordered them to come back.

"Jack." Paige kept her tone soft as she approached, not wanting him to explode on her again. "Is everything okay? They look like they are safe."

"For now. The tide comes in fast here."

"Then they'll get on their boards and come home. I'm sure it will be fine."

It was not fine.

Twenty minutes later, the tide had taken their paddles away and everyone was clutching their boards as the waterline crept up to their knees. Horatio was waving his arms in the air and facing the beach.

"Help! Help! Our paddles are gone!"

"An absolute dipshit." Jack swore as he strode to the dinghy and jumped in. The rest of the retreat had all gathered close together on the beach to watch the drama unfold. Horatio, knowing he had an audience, started ordering his little group of yogis around. Soon, all four of them were crouched, kneeling on their paddleboards, trying to paddle forward with their hands. Jack had been right. The tide had come in fast and now the sand bar had disappeared completely. Not to mention, the waves had picked up, careening into the paddleboards and causing each person to clutch the side of the board to keep from falling into the ocean.

"Throw me the line." Jack gestured to a pile of rope wrapped around a bracket on the dock. Paige raced forward and unwound it, tossing it into the boat.

"Do you need my help?"

"I've got it." Jack started the engine and reversed from the dock, turning the soft dinghy around so that it was facing where the sand bar had been.

Worry raced through her as another set of waves pummeled the paddleboarders. They were outside the protected cove area. If someone got knocked off, would they be contending with currents? Paige watched as Jack reached the group quickly, cutting the engine as he drifted closer. She saw him gesturing with his hands and wondered how he planned to handle this. The boat wasn't big enough to fit the people and the paddleboards, but if Jack only rescued the people then the paddleboards would be a loss. Having studied the expense of ordering goods to the island, Paige was well aware what a costly decision that would be.

"Why's he always gotta be showing off like that?" Stan, one of the men who regularly showed off for Mariposa each night, griped to her.

"The universe only knows," Paige said.

"He should've listened to Jack."

"And to me. I also advised him against going out there," Paige pointed out.

"Yeah, but Horatio never listens to you."

Stung, Paige turned away and was surprised to feel the prick of tears at her eyes. She knew it was just an offhand

comment, but that's what made it worse. It was a reality
that everyone around her had accepted long ago and something that had taken being slapped upside the head with her
bed full of yoga beauties to finally see. Why had she
allowed someone to treat her like that for so long? It
wasn't particularly gratifying to find that others viewed her
as a doormat as well.

Now, as she watched Horatio argue with Jack, she realized once again what a contrast the two men were. Jack
listened to her opinions and allowed her to make decisions
and never seemed threatened when she took charge in a
situation. Because of that, she often was happy to defer to
him in situations where she knew he had more knowledge.
It was a respectful working relationship. Whereas her relationship with Horatio had been...Paige's stomach clenched
as she watched Horatio cross his arms over his chest on his
paddleboard in a huff and then almost proceed to fall off
the board. She'd pampered him, Paige realized. She'd
acted like his damn maid because that is what he'd
demanded of her. Horatio had never viewed her as a partner. Instead he'd viewed her like the hired help with an
added bonus of sex on the side. Here she'd thought that
she'd been in charge and running everything, when in
reality Horatio had been manipulating her all along.

"Maybe if he had listened, he wouldn't be stuck up shit
creek without a paddle." Paige found herself saying to the
guest. Never had there been a time when that particular
saying was more appropriate, Paige thought, as she
scanned the horizon for the missing paddles.

"That's true. The studio's not running so smoothly
since you left. Even if Horatio treated you like crap, you

still did a good job managing everything," Stan said. Paige was surprised but pleased with the compliment.

"Thanks, Stan. I really liked working there. I thought I did a good job."

"You did. The business lost a good asset in you. But I'd say you landed on your feet just fine." With that, Stan walked to the end of the dock to get a better view of the debacle. Paige hadn't expected to find an epiphany coming from the mouth of one middle-aged half-hearted yogi, but nevertheless, here she was. Because Stan was right. She could beat herself up for her relationship with Horatio, but she couldn't fault her work ethic or what she'd accomplished at her job. While she'd certainly had to accept some personal lessons when it came to her choices, she'd also learned a lot and grown in her business acumen. For that, she could be grateful. A sense of peace washed through her, easing the tension from her shoulders, and she walked slowly forward to see how Jack was handling this situation.

He'd thrown a rope to the group and had each person pass it back to the next. Paige realized he was going to tow the group slowly in so that they could stay on their boards. Paige held her breath as he started the engine and began the tedious and awkward trek back to the dock. The group looked grateful for the help, keeping their eyes focused on the task at hand. But when they drew near to the dock, Horatio, perched on the last board in the group, looked up and saw everybody watching. Never one to miss an audience, he propped himself up on his knees, and then wobbled himself to a standing position as Jack drew in line with the dock.

"You see, my followers? You can do yoga anywhere. Yoga isn't just about the movements. It's about the mindset and clearing the blockages to your energy." With that, Horatio bent forward to attempt a warrior three pose. He overcalculated, misbalanced, and in an unfortunate or fortunate timing of events, depending on who was watching, tipped over and hit the side of his face into the dock before disappearing underwater.

"Horatio!" Nadia screamed.

"Damn it." Jack swore and looked up at the dock. Spying Paige, he cut the engine, tossed her the line, and dove into the water in one seamless motion. Paige caught the line and tied the boat, her heart hammering in her chest as she waited for Jack to surface.

She hadn't actually wanted Horatio to die when she'd wished he'd float off to sea. Paige had just hoped he'd not…be around here anymore. But still alive. Just somewhere else. When Jack broke the surface with a flailing Horatio in his arms, everyone cheered.

Jack swam awkwardly to the ladder and handed Horatio off. The dripping yoga instructor pulled himself up the ladder and deposited himself on the dock.

"Oh, Jack. You're a hero!" Nadia crowed and soon they were all cheering for Jack.

Paige didn't miss the sullen look that clouded Horatio's face and moved forward to crouch next to him.

"Let me check you for injuries."

"I'm fine. It was nothing," Horatio bit out, pushing her hand away and trying to stand.

"Just give it a second. You've had a shock and probably swallowed some sea water."

"I said I'm fine, Paige. Why are you being so pushy?"

"Because you have a knot the size of a goose egg on your face, and it's my job to make sure you don't die on me, much to my chagrin."

"Anger doesn't become you. If you'd taken any of my classes this week, you could've cleared that energy," Horatio had the gall to point out to Paige as she touched his face. He winced when she pressed a bit too hard on his wound.

"I didn't ask for your advice, Horatio. Nor do I need it. We'll need to get some ice on your face. If you think you can stand, we can get you to the reception hall."

"I said I'm fine." With that, Horatio stood and stormed down the dock, while the rest of the group looked after him in surprise. Jack shot him a glare from where he was busy stacking the paddleboards back on the beach.

"Do you need me to help with anything?" Paige asked, striding down the dock to Jack.

"Storm's brewing with that one. I'd say get him an ice pack and a rum punch. I'm going back out after the paddles."

"But…won't it be impossible to find them?"

Paige looked back to where Horatio stormed across the beach, Nadia and Lily on his heels. He was her past, Paige realized, and, well, while she didn't know what her future held yet, she did know one thing.

Jack always took care of everyone else. Maybe it was time to take care of him.

"I'm coming with you." Paige hopped in the boat before he could protest.

CHAPTER TWENTY-TWO

"Are you sure you don't need to tend to the man-baby? He is likely to be kicking up quite a fuss right now." Jack's tone was harsh as he walked the dinghy back out into deeper water.

"You mean our primary guest who you've advised me to attend to with the utmost care?" Paige reminded Jack, keeping her tone light, but also refusing to let him be a jerk to her.

"Ah, fuck it. You're right. You really should go to him. I've got this."

"It'll be easier with two people. Plus, Horatio has plenty of people to see to his needs."

Jack hopped in the boat and took his position by the motor. She watched as he lowered the engine back into the water and started it, reversing them smoothly before turning the dinghy around. They motored slowly in silence for a moment, and Paige took a moment to calm her emotions while scanning the water for the paddles. Jack had annoyed her, but she could understand his frustration.

"I'm sorry."

"What's that?" Paige turned, unsure if she'd heard him correctly. Jack grimaced and then shrugged his tanned shoulders at her.

"I said I was sorry. I'm just frustrated and I shouldn't have taken it out on you. The idiot nearly got himself killed. And that's on me."

"No, Jack. That's on him. We both warned him of the danger. Didn't you tell me that this wasn't a kid's camp? They are adults, remember? He just makes shitty decisions. He does this all the time. Horatio likes to feel like he is in charge, and I think he's threatened by you."

"By me? Why? I'm the last person who is going to compete with him for yoga guru status," Jack laughed. "I like to lift weights and swim. That's the extent of my workouts."

"Well, they do well by you," Paige let her eyes trail over the muscles on his abdomen. She licked her lips. "Very well."

"Thank you. Though, I can't knock yoga. You are mighty fit, Miss Paige."

"Thank you. I'm bendy, too," Paige shot a grin over her shoulder and then turned to look back out at the waves before she did something stupid like clamber across the boat and jump him. "Tell me what to look for."

"If we're lucky, they'll still be tied in a bundle. Otherwise, it's gonna be tough to spot them. The paddles were black with yellow at the ends. So, just look for any ripple in the surface, and we'll see if we can collect them."

"I'm sorry, I know this is annoying." Paige dropped to

her knees and pressed her stomach against the soft side of the dinghy so as to better see the surface of the water.

"It is. But I don't want to order new paddles, and it's more unnecessary waste in the ocean. If we're lucky, we'll only be out a little bit of time."

"And, I can't say I mind being out here with you rather than back there dealing with him," Paige said.

"I don't blame you for that."

They fell into companionable silence as they searched, and Paige found herself enjoying the boat ride. The sun warmed her and the breeze rippled over the waves, cooling her skin.

"There they are!" Paige pointed excitedly to the paddles floating ahead of them. "I see them!"

"Nice spot. Keep an eye on them." Jack increased their speed until they reached the paddles, circling the boat nicely so that Paige could lean over and grab the bundle. Heaving them into the boat, she laughed as she almost hit Jack in the head with them.

"Whoops."

"I probably deserved that."

"No you didn't. You were frustrated. You take care of a lot of things around here. I am sure it gets exhausting. I guess…I want to be able to help you, is all."

"That's…" Jack blew out a breath. "That's nice, Paige. That's actually nice as hell. I don't think anyone ever really offers to help me."

"Well, do you ask for help?"

Jack slanted her a look before starting the engine again.

"Typical man." Paige muttered this low enough that he wouldn't hear, but he must have caught her meaning because a grin flashed across his face. This time, Jack turned up the speed and they bounced across the water, the salty spray of waves misting her face.

"Look!" Paige cried, almost toppling out of the boat as she forgot herself and tried to stand.

"The dolphins," Jack slowed the boat. "This pod has been coming by lately."

"Oh, Jack!" Paige bent over the front of the bow. "They have a baby with them!"

Sure enough, a pod of sleek gray dolphins danced just below the surface, keeping time with the boat, as they surfaced periodically in the waves. Paige's heart trembled in her chest, as the tiniest dolphin, surrounded by her family, seemed to laugh up at her from the turquoise waters.

"Do you think they know we're here? Like on the boat?" Paige called.

"I think they like to have fun. I'd normally let you swim with them, but not with a baby around."

"Why?"

"They're protective. As soon as you jump in, they'll dive deep. Otherwise, if you sing and dance in the water they'll come over."

"Shut up," Paige laughed, delighted at the thought. "They do not."

"They do! I swear. They are playful, and I think they must wonder what these idiots are doing jerking around in the water and yodeling."

"I love it. I love them!" Paige couldn't get enough of the pod that kept time with the boat. "Oh, can't we stay with them a little bit longer?"

"Of course we can. Your wish is my command."

Paige smiled back at him before bending over the front of the boat to watch the dolphins dance in the waves. He couldn't know what those words meant to her. Nobody had really put her first before. It was something so simple really, drawing out the experience so that she could enjoy this time with the dolphins.

But she'd never forget this moment – or the man who had made it possible.

CHAPTER TWENTY-THREE

They all drank that night.

"The ex okay?" Mariposa asked as she pulled out liquor bottles and held them in the air, making notes on a little pad in front of her.

"Seems to be. I think his pride is hurt more than anything. Though he'll likely have a bruise."

"Jack had to rescue them, I heard."

"He did. And then the idiot over there decides to try to…" Paige was shocked when a laugh bubbled up her throat. "Tried to…" She pushed her mouth together, not wanting to break out in laughter, but the effort proved too much. It was like when she was supposed to be quiet during a serious occasion and no matter how hard she tried, Paige could not stop. Tears streamed down her cheeks as she gasped, waving a hand in front of her face, turning her body so that Horatio couldn't see her expression across the reception hall. A wide grin broke out on the beautiful bartender's face. "He…Jack…pulled them back on the dinghy."

"Go on." Mariposa gestured, clearly enjoying Paige's attempt to contain her giggles.

"And…and…" A snort escaped and Paige slapped a hand over her mouth, bending her head to the bar. "The idiot decides to try a yoga pose as Jack pulled up to the dock."

"On a moving paddle board?" Mariposa's eyes rounded.

"Yes," Paige gasped.

"I'm guessing that is how he got the bruise?"

"Just…kerplat!" Paige clapped her hands together, her shoulders shaking. "He just…face…first…dock."

"That's his own damn fault then. You know, for a moment I was feeling bad for him." Mariposa chuckled. She was smart enough to keep her eyes on the bottles she was inventorying and not look across the hall at Horatio.

"Don't…" Paige gasped, wiping her eyes. "Just don't. This one is all his fault."

"I think you deserve a drink after that one." Mariposa slid her a rum punch in a tiki mug, and Paige accepted it gratefully. She took a sip of the sweet fruity drink and schooled her breathing.

"There's the hero himself."

Paige looked up as Jack joined them at the bar, a grumpy look on his handsome face.

"Beer," Jack said, and then his tone softened. "Please."

"I was going to say…" Mariposa gave him a look.

"Sorry. I'm…"

"Annoyed that Horatio is acting like he meant to do this? That discomfort is a growth tool?" A giggle escaped and Jack turned to Paige, narrowing his eyes.

"Is that how he is spinning it?" Jack's tone was anything but pleased.

"I understand. Trust me, I get it." Paige tried to hold back the laughter again. "It's just...did you see...when he..."

"If he hadn't hit his head on the dock, I was going to do it for him." Jack took a slug of his beer.

"And then...just..." Paige made a motion with her hands. "Splash!"

"I honestly contemplated leaving him there." A begrudging smile worked its way onto Jack's face.

"Bad for the hotel's image." Paige shook her head sadly.

"But oh so satisfying." The tension eased from Jack's face, and this time he smiled for real.

"Not much longer, guys. Head's up...they're coming," Mariposa said, her tone low, and a bright, welcoming smile on her face.

"Did you get the paddles?" Stan asked, slapping Jack on the back. He'd changed for dinner, and Paige looked around to realize most people had done the same.

"I did. Luckily." Jack hoisted his beer.

"I'll be right back, I just need to freshen up." Paige took her tiki drink and hightailed it from the reception hall and the group that had surrounded the bar. Even though island life was casual, it wouldn't reflect well on her to show up to dinner covered in sand. She'd taken her cue from CeCe and Whit on this one, since each night they appeared dressed to the nines as though they were hosting a fancy dinner party.

Paige took a quick shower, bundling her hair on top of

her head and rinsing the sand from her legs. After toweling off, she stood under the little air conditioner for a moment, letting the puffs of cool air soothe her warm skin as her thoughts drifted to Jack.

She was falling hard, Paige realized.

The moment today with the dolphins hung suspended in her mind – a crystalline moment of perfection where she knew she was exactly where she wanted to be with a person she enjoyed being with. Even though Jack had times where he was quite broody, and even though Paige had yet to figure out some of the undercurrents between him and the others, she found herself looking to him more often than not. Jack carried himself with a confidence that just seemed to say – no matter what the problem was – he could handle it. It was such a contrast to Horatio's incessant need to have other people take care of his problems that it was like Paige had been held hostage in a dark cave and was seeing the light of day for the first time in years.

And yes, Paige knew that she shouldn't have feelings for a co-worker. She *knew* it. She'd already lectured herself more than once – in the depths of the nights when she'd wake up after another sweaty dream about Jack – do *not* sleep with the boss.

But, damn she wanted to. Their stolen kiss from the other night haunted her.

Sighing, Paige dug through her closet and pulled out a dress she hadn't worn yet. It was a deep red, with turquoise shimmers splashed across it. The neckline was low, the dress hugged her curves, and the hemline ended just above her knees. Now that she had more of a tan, the red looked good against her skin. Paige pulled her hair down and shook it out, letting it tumble down her back in a cloud of curls, and hooked some big silver dangles in her ears.

Jack always complimented her, Paige realized as she studied herself in the mirror. He was respectful to her, complimented her on her work, and complimented her on her outfits. He never crossed the line, so she didn't feel uncomfortable when he did comment on her appearance, and Paige respected how he managed boundaries. But now she kind of wanted him to cross some lines with her.

She liked how they talked. Their conversations were only snippets, moments caught here and there in between handling the guests, but the topics were varied and interesting. They talked about books, travels, music, and life experiences. Over the past couple weeks, Paige had started to piece together a picture of a man who was well-traveled, well-read, and comfortably confident in his place in the world.

And…she needed to stop thinking about him, Paige realized. It would only make her crush worse, and she was well aware that her tendency to give in to her impulses was what often landed her in tricky situations. Giving herself a stern lecture, Paige downed the rest of her rum punch and left the cottage. Immediately, she missed the cool air of her room as the heat pressed against her skin. Paige paused for a moment, just outside the reception hall and took a good look around.

Various lights were scattered through the walkways that wound to the different cottages, lighting the palm trees from below, and creating a warm ambiance at night. The breeze ruffled the palm fronds, and the waves crashed in the background. The ocean had become a background sound that Paige had now gotten used to, and she wondered if she'd miss it when she left. Tiki torches lined the outside of the open-air reception, fire dancing in the darkness, and the guests laughed and chattered around the bar and at various tables. The mood was light, everything was moving along smoothly, and Paige felt truly at ease for the first time since she'd landed on Poco Poco Island.

What could possibly go wrong now?

Horatio's accident seemed to have set off a mood of celebration, Paige realized, as everyone drank more than usual that night, herself included. For once, Paige let her hair down a bit and drank rum punch after rum punch. As the night took on a fuzzy quality, Paige couldn't decide if Mariposa was making her drinks weaker or if she was just not tasting the alcohol anymore.

"Water." Mariposa handed her a bottle. It was an order, not a question and Paige accepted the bottle gratefully, downing it in one go.

"Thank you."

"One more." Mariposa handed her another.

Paige sobered a bit, leaning back against the bar and watching the group. Dinner had been a success, with a delicious taco bar that had caused CeCe to roll her eyes. But Paige had noticed that didn't stop the woman from enjoying three tacos herself. The dinner had been spent with everyone praising Jack for being a hero, and Horatio's expression growing mutinous. Now, the group had urged them to turn the music up and a dance party had ensued.

Sunday was a free day with no classes scheduled, so Paige didn't bother to try to rein anyone in. If they wanted to cut loose tonight, so be it. CeCe's raucous laugh caused

Paige to turn and her eyebrows shot up. Locked in a decidedly steamy embrace, CeCe and Stan were attempting what looked to be a tango, but they were both so drunk that they were pretty much just falling all over each other and laughing. That didn't stop their enthusiasm though, as CeCe tried to hook a leg around Stan's waist, and Stan tried to lift her so that she could sit on his waist. Unable to bear watching them fall, Paige turned and caught Jack's dark look at CeCe before he turned away.

Whit, of course, was nowhere to be seen. Why didn't that man look after his wife? Paige wondered. All of a sudden, she grew weary of the party.

"I'm going to tuck in, unless you think you'll need me?"

"Go on." Mariposa nodded. "We've got two security guards on tonight and Luis stuck around. Jack will also do pass-throughs. I'm good. We always put extra people on for Saturday nights."

"Smart. This crowd might be up for a while."

"I close the bar at twelve-thirty. They won't have a choice after that." Mariposa grinned at her and wiggled her fingers in goodbye as Paige slipped away. She padded softly to her cottage, enjoying the gentle breeze, and swaying slightly with the alcohol that was still in her system. She'd just gone inside her cottage when a voice surprised her, causing her to slam her hand against her chest.

"Horatio!" Paige took a deep breath. "What are you doing here? You scared me."

Horatio came into her cottage and closed the door behind him, like he had every right to do so. Annoyed,

Paige crossed the room and opened the door back up, not caring if the cool air got out. She didn't want Horatio to stay and she certainly didn't want anyone passing by to think she'd invited Horatio into her space.

"What's with that Jack guy?" Horatio paced the room, his arms crossed and annoyance lacing his tone. "He thinks he's the man or something."

"Um, I highly doubt that."

"Oh sure, you would defend him."

"I'm just saying that I don't think you can assume what anyone else is thinking of themselves. Isn't that what the ego is?" Paige parroted some of Horatio's own words back to him.

"He deliberately tries to show me up. This is *my* retreat. My followers. They should be listening to *my* words."

"Um, this is Yoga Soulone's retreat hosted by Tranquila Inn. Jack is part of making sure this goes smoothly." Paige stood in her doorway, her arms crossed.

"What he's trying to do is be in charge."

"Well, he kind of is."

"He's making me look like a fool!" Horatio, for the first time ever, looked truly angry. Not like when he put on a temper tantrum or had a meltdown, but fully angry. Paige wondered how much he'd had to drink as a ripple of apprehension went through her.

"The only one making you look like a fool is yourself." Her tone was clipped as she gestured for the door. "And I think it's time for you to leave."

"I miss you, Paige. We were good together, baby." The sudden switch in topics had Paige confused for a moment.

Which is the only reason she didn't immediately shove Horatio away when his lips descended on hers. Hadn't he just been bitching about Jack? As Horatio moaned low in his throat and pulled her to him, Paige shook herself from her daze and pushed her hands against his chest, and ripped her lips from his.

"I asked you to leave," Paige gritted out, pushing harder against his chest, though his arms were like a vice clamp around her.

"Come on, baby. You know you loved our time in bed. Don't you miss us?"

"I really *truly* don't. Please leave." Paige could see now just how drunk Horatio was and that worried her. Her heart rate kicked up as she struggled in Horatio's arms.

"Shouldn't we give it one more chance?"

"The lady said no."

Paige closed her eyes as relief washed over her at Jack's words. Which was immediately followed by distress, because if she knew anything about Horatio at all, it was that he wasn't going to back down without a fight.

"And what are you going to do about it?" Horatio released Paige, turning to square up to Jack. They stood just outside her cottage, dark silhouettes lit from the tiki torches behind them. One man sinewy and lean, the other all muscle. Paige knew in a heartbeat that Jack would win in a fight.

"I just did something about it," Jack said, his tone even. But Paige saw him rock lightly back on his feet, his palms held loosely open. He was ready for whatever Horatio would try.

"You know you don't have to run to everyone's rescue? This has nothing to do with you."

"It's my job to make sure guests and employees get home safe." Jack kept his tone even.

"She's safe."

"Are *you*?" Jack asked.

"What's that supposed to mean?"

"You're clearly in the wrong cabin. I'm worried you won't find your way back to your cottage. You wouldn't want to get stuck out here all night with the bugs."

"I…" Horatio looked around.

"I think Nadia was looking for you, Horatio. Right, Jack?" Paige spoke softly, not wanting to draw Jack's attention in case Horatio suddenly made a move.

"She was. She wants to go to bed. I said I'd come find you. I'm sure you'd like to go to her, wouldn't you, bud?"

"Yes, I do. She's much better in bed than you ever were." Horatio spit at Paige before stomping off into the darkness. Paige turned, tears filling her eyes, and she rushed for the bathroom to splash cool water over her face. The taste of Horatio was still in her mouth, so she vigorously brushed her teeth as she tried to push the embarrassment that burned in her core away. It didn't matter what Horatio thought of her performance in bed, Paige told herself.

But she *hated* that Jack had to hear that. Or think that of her. After she toweled her face off, Paige bracketed her hands on the sink and looked in the mirror. It didn't matter what any man thought of her, she told herself. The only opinion that mattered was her own. And Paige was proud of herself for taking risks and working hard. Nobody could take that from her. Screw Horatio, she thought, as she left the bathroom. He would be something she would laugh about someday.

"You okay?"

"Oh shit," Paige stopped and held a hand to her heart for the second time. "People really need to stop scaring me in my cottage."

"I hope I don't scare you." Jack leaned against the wall, his arms crossed over his chest, a concerned look on his handsome face. Paige couldn't help but notice the way his muscles bulged in his arms. Stay focused on the conversation, she ordered herself, as her mind began to wander in a much naughtier direction.

"*You* don't. Just surprised me is all." Paige walked across the room to stand in front of him. Her cottage was small with no place to sit other than on the bed.

"Are you okay?" Jack asked again. He searched her eyes.

"I…yeah, I am. Just…"

"He was trying to hurt you."

"He was. His ego is bruised and he lashed out."

"Doesn't make it right." Jack shifted on his feet, dropping his arms and clenching his fists.

"No, it doesn't." Paige smiled and tucked a strand of hair behind her ear. "It really doesn't. And despite all I tell myself about what an idiot he is…his words still hurt."

"I would think that if anyone was bad in bed, it's him."

Paige surprised herself by laughing. "Why would you say that?"

"Because men who only think about themselves don't care about a woman's pleasure."

"Oh." The air in the room seemed to thicken around them, and Paige found herself caught in Jack's gaze. "I… you're absolutely right."

"Did he ever please you, Paige?" Jack's words were soft.

"No…" Paige licked her lips. "No. He…honestly, it was all about him."

"Maybe it's time it was all about you."

CHAPTER TWENTY-FOUR

Paige kissed him.

Because what else was a girl supposed to do when a man she was attracted to said something like that to her? Maybe it was the rum punch. Maybe it was her adrenaline still humming from fending off Horatio.

And maybe it was just because she wanted to.

There was something about these late hours in the night, when the pulse of the island picked up, and the beat of the waves pounded in rhythm with the island. Paige could feel it in her core, this deep-rooted wanting, this knowing…that Jack would be hers tonight. When his arms came around her, heat throbbed thickly through her, lust fueling her veins, and she wound her arms around his neck.

He kissed her like a warrior staking claim to a castle.

Like anything Jack did, he put his full attention to it and saw the job through. Kissing was no different. Paige moaned against his mouth as Jack tilted his head, deepening the kiss, and his hands began to stroke lightly over her back, down her sides, and stopping just at her waist. They never wandered, only stroking lightly, never taking liberties that weren't yet given. It was this restraint that made Paige want more from him. She wanted to see those careful threads of control snap; she wanted to see him come undone.

And she wanted to be the one to do it to him.

Paige dug her hands into Jack's hair, pulling him closer, sighing as her body pressed to his. She rubbed herself against him, her softness and curves meeting a wall of rock-hard muscle. Jack teased her with his tongue, dipping in for a taste, kissing her like he had all the time in the world. His hands continued to stroke her back lightly – soothing her, slowing her down. Where she wanted to run, he wanted to stroll. It drove the heat that tugged low in her body to a frenzy, and Paige gasped against his lips, tugging him back toward the bed.

Jack broke the embrace and turned to the door, and Paige let out a little mewl of distress.

"Just making sure we don't have any unwanted visitors." Jack sent her a devastating smile as he locked the door and turned back to her. Lust pooled low in Paige's stomach at the click of the lock, and she reached for the hem of her dress.

"Oh no. Please, allow me." Jack stepped forward and Paige dropped her hands, smiling up at him. "Do you know I've been thinking about doing this since the day you landed at the hotel?"

"No?" Paige laughed, surprised that he'd been attracted to her from the beginning.

"Oh, yes," Jack said, tracing his lips across her neck.

"There you were. All these curves packed into uncomfortable clothes. Annoyed and uncertain. I wanted you to leave."

"You were pretty clear on that." Paige pulled back for a moment to meet his eyes. "You weren't very welcoming. Why did you want me to leave?"

"Because I knew I wanted to do this…" Jack surprised her by kissing his way down her neck to her cleavage. He licked once at the side of her breast, causing Paige to gasp as his hands trailed up and down her sides. "And I knew that I shouldn't."

"Oh…" The power of speech had been robbed from Paige as his hands continued down to the hem of her dress. Jack continued to press soft kisses to the skin of her cleavage and she felt her body go loose, her nipples swelling at his touch, her mind screaming for release.

"May I?" Jack asked as he tugged at the fabric of her dress.

"Oh, please do." Nope, her power of speech was still there. "Jack…I…"

"Yes, Paige?"

Jack stopped, tilting his head to look up at her. Blue eyes heated with lust speared her.

"Don't stop."

"Thank god." Jack breathed and pulled the dress slowly up Paige's body, tantalizing them both as he revealed her shape to him. Paige had only a skimpy lace thong on, as the halter style of the dress hadn't allowed for a bra. Now, as the cool air hit her skin, Paige was grateful for one less piece of clothing between them. Speaking of…

"You, too," Paige said and reached out to tug at Jack's shirt. "I want to see you."

"What the lady wants…" Jack tore his shirt off and tossed it across the room, causing Paige to chuckle. But then the laugh caught in her throat when Jack's mouth found her skin again. Reaching out, Paige gripped his arms as her head fell back, and Jack began to worship her body. He continued to kiss her gently, not yet touching her breasts, only kissing soft circles around them, whispering decadent words of delight against her skin. The delay was driving her crazy.

"Jack…please…" Paige moaned, wanting him to touch her fully.

"Please what?" Jack asked, blowing softly on one nipple and causing every nerve ending in Paige's body to scream for attention.

"Touch me." It was a whisper. It was a plea. It was a benediction.

When Jack's mouth closed over Paige's nipple, she bowed back. When she would have fallen onto the bed, Jack's arm caught her, pulling her tight against him as he worshipped her breasts with his mouth. Over and over, Jack kissed her, his lips trailing a damp path across her skin, her body heating to his touch. She squirmed, wanting him more than ever, and gasped as he brought his head up to find her lips once more.

"I want you," Paige panted against his mouth, pulling him until she tumbled back onto the bed and he followed, anchoring himself on his arms over her.

"You're so beautiful, Paige," Jack said, his expression soft as he kneeled and ran one hand down the side of her body and over her thighs. Paige automatically widened her legs, craving his touch. "Your body is a dream. All these hills and curves. I could touch you for days."

"Please, don't stop." Paige trembled as he traced his hands down the soft skin of her inner thigh, finding a sensitive spot behind her knee, and surprising her when he scraped his teeth lightly over that spot. Her hips bracketed off the bed at that, and Jack chuckled, continuing to work his way down her legs, trailing his hands down to her ankles, his touch whisper soft.

She'd never had a man take this much time with her before, Paige realized, and was shocked to find herself all but panting in need. What was he doing down at her ankles when she wanted him inside her...now? The heat that had built low in her body threatened to burst, and Paige whimpered as Jack's mouth found the delicate skin of her inner thigh.

"Do you like when I kiss you here?" Jack said, his breath soft against her skin, making her shiver because his mouth was so close to where she wanted him most.

"Yes," Paige gasped and tried to pull him closer with her legs. Jack smiled, pushing her legs wider, before capturing her wrist with one hand and pinning it to the bed. He kissed his way higher on her thigh, before hovering over where she ached for him. Her hips jerked as he blew on her, his laughter at her response only deepening her need.

"What about here?" Jack asked, finding her most tender spot and sucking gently. Paige bowed back as lust exploded, waves of pleasure and years of pent-up anxiety rocketing through her, and Jack caught her hips, pulling her to his mouth, deftly riding the storm as she convulsed around him.

"Wait...wait..." Paige moaned, her nerve endings over-sensitized. Jack pulled back, blowing lightly on her, giving her a moment to collect herself.

"Now?" Jack asked, sending her a devasting smile, before bending his head and finding her once more with his tongue. Paige moaned as liquid heat washed through her, his tongue swirling over her, tasting, testing, and pushing her over the edge once more in such delicious heat that Paige sat up and grabbed Jack's shoulders, dragging him to her.

"I need...I need..." Paige said, finding his mouth, tasting herself on him, and kissing him deeply as he settled over her. "I want to touch you."

"One second, beautiful." Jack pulled back and rummaged in his shorts. Her mouth dropped open as he took the rest of his clothes off, and she saw another reason why he carried himself with such confidence. After he protected himself with a condom, Jack leaned back over her, bracketing his arms on either side of her shoulders. "Now...what was this about touching me?"

"I want to..." Paige threw her head back as his hard length found her, rubbing itself against her heat, teasing her most sensitive spot. "Touch. You. Too."

"You are." Jack grinned as he captured her mouth and in one long thrust he entered her, filling her to the core, his kisses capturing her cries.

He didn't just take. He demanded. Matching him thrust for thrust, Paige lifted her hips to his, his hardness filling her – soothing her – taking her like nothing had before.

Desire careened through her as she clenched around him, drawing him deeper, liquid heat meeting hard steel.

They arrived at the same place together, both crying out as they fell over the edge into bliss, their bodies moving in harmony. When it was over, Jack stayed where he was, pinning her with his weight as he trailed soft kisses over her face and down her neck. Despite having just been very thoroughly satisfied, Paige found her need for him had not yet abated.

"I didn't get to touch you as much as I wanted to."

"Oh, by all means then…be my guest," Jack said with a devastating smile.

And Paige did just that.

CHAPTER TWENTY-FIVE

Paige stretched as the first light of morning filtered softly into her bedroom. The only sounds that greeted her were the soft hum of the air conditioning and the chorus of the island birds as they began to greet the day. Rolling, Paige reached across the bed and was met with…blankets. Pushing herself up on one elbow, she stared blearily at the empty space next to her. Certain they'd fallen asleep entwined together, Paige plopped back to her pillow and stared at the white-washed planks of the ceiling.

He'd left without saying goodbye.

Misgivings slipped through her stomach, and she grabbed the other pillow, pulling it over her face and breathing his scent in. Everything was fine, Paige told herself. While they had both been drinking, Paige was certain she'd had her wits about her as had Jack. The decisions they made were their own, and something they would both have to live with. Paige only hoped that it wouldn't be awkward…this…well, whatever the two of them were.

Maybe it was best to take it slow. Paige laughed into the pillow as she thought about all the ways Jack had pleasured her the night before. Okay, so they hadn't taken that part slow. But she wasn't ready to move in and be a partner to somebody again like she had been with Horatio. Granted, she was already living at Tranquila Inn, but this wasn't the same situation.

It wasn't, she scolded herself and rolled from the bed. This was…it was just for fun. That was it. That was all it could or would be. Just fun and easy and nothing more. Paige forced her giddy mind away from imagining what a future with Jack would look like. Nope, not going there. Paige stretched again as she stood next to the bed and glanced at the clock. It was still terribly early. Knowing that most of the guests wouldn't be up for hours yet – what with all the mad partying from the night before – Paige decided she would try for a little self-care and do a yoga practice on her own. It had been weeks since she'd done any sort of yoga, and while she didn't miss Horatio, she could tell her body missed the daily movements of the yoga stretches.

Paige pulled on a sports bra, yoga shorts, and tucked a rolled yoga mat under her arm. Deciding she wanted the fresh air and the ocean this morning, she left her cottage and veered away from the main beach, wandering through the other cottages and toward the outskirts of the property. She rarely came this way, as it was where CeCe and Whit lived in their double-room cottage. Paige paused when she saw the front door to the cottage open and heard voices.

The hair on the back of her neck rose, and she ducked behind a bush, peering between the leaves at the front of clapboard white cottage.

Jack stood in the doorway, naked to the waist, his shirt in hand.

Paige's stomach dropped when CeCe wrapped an arm around his waist and leaned in, pressing her head against his shoulder.

"I love you," CeCe sighed.

Paige didn't wait to see any more. Instead, she dashed back the way she had come, her stomach roiling. When she saw Luis waving to her from where he knelt by a hedge, Paige waved back and veered to the right, all but running for the beach. Once there, she picked up her pace into a light jog, her feet slamming into the hard-packed sand on the water's edge, and she ran until Tranquila Inn was just a speck in the distance. Finally, with sweat pouring down her back, she dropped her yoga mat on the sand and plopped down onto it.

She blinked at the tears that made her vision fuzzy, dug her toes into the sand, and forced herself to work on repetitive breaths until she could bring her heart rate down. It did nothing for the panic that laced her stomach, but eventually, her pulse settled and her eyes cleared. A little bird, picking its way along the sand, paused in front of her and tilted its head to study her as if it wondered what this strange creature was doing in its breakfast spot.

"I don't know what I'm doing here either."

She'd done it again, Paige realized. Jumped too fast. Made impulsive decisions. And here she was, having been played for a fool. It all made sense now – the constant annoyance that Jack had with CeCe. The broody looks and the familiarity. Though they were decades apart, they were clearly an item. No wonder Mariposa had told Paige not to comment on Whit's nightly disappearances with the ladies. Clearly, there was some sort of weird arrangement that everyone had an understanding of but her. Once again, Paige had been left in the dark.

What an idiot she was.

No matter how much Jack claimed he hated Horatio, Jack was just the same. Sleeping with women to get what he wanted. Hadn't CeCe bankrolled him in other jobs through the years? He was clearly her boytoy, and Paige had chosen to look past the deep-rooted familiarity with those two.

Grinding her teeth, Paige tried to stop the next wave of tears that threatened. Damn it. She'd liked Jack. As in, *really* liked him. How could she have been so stupid?

"Because you saw what you wanted to see," Paige said out loud and the bird bounced a few feet away from her, startled by her voice. Paige hugged her arms around her knees and looked out at the water.

The ocean was calm today, almost eerily so. Paige wondered if the water was always this still this early in the morning or if it was just today. The water moved gently, almost like glass, and no big waves rolled into the shoreline. There was no wind, and Paige brushed at the occasional bug that landed on her legs. The sky reflected Paige's mood – a gloomy gray with just a faint tinge of pink where the horizon met the water.

"Okay," Paige said, "Okay, okay, okay. So this happened. *It happened.* You wanted to jump him – so you did. It is not your fault he was involved with someone else. That's on him. You didn't do anything wrong. Other than jump your boss, of course. Which you'd promised you wouldn't do because things were going to be different this time. So what have we learned? You have impulse problems. And you're likely working out your anger with Horatio by looking to Jack to save you. To redeem you. But the only person that can do that is you. So from this point on, you stop looking elsewhere for the love that only you can give yourself."

Self-reflection was a bitch sometimes.

Unfortunately, she wasn't wrong. Paige realized that nobody was going to solve her problems or fill any gaping holes of unworthiness inside her but herself. And that would likely be a long-term job. In the meantime, if she could just manage to not jump into any other impulsive situations, maybe she could take a year off and focus on her own personal growth. Starting with getting off this island. There was no way she'd be able to stay on with what she'd discovered this morning. Though it made her sad – gutted her, really – it felt like the right decision. It burned though, as she'd come to like her weird little island family and Jack most of all. Blinking back the tears that threatened again, Paige shuddered in a deep breath.

Decided, Paige nodded to herself and stood. Since she was here, she might as well do some of her practice. The sky had moved from moody gray to shell pink, and Paige moved through a series of Sun Salutations. By the time she was finished, the sun was just cresting the horizon at her back and Paige knew it was time to return to Tranquila Inn. Holding her head high, she walked back instead of running, following the path of her footprints in the sand. The water hadn't rolled up to wash her prints away, and Paige wondered if this was the lowest point of low tide. She hadn't been out to the ocean in the mornings yet – perhaps it was always low tide at this time. A flock of birds startled her as they squawked past her, careening in a frenzied mass, and darted inland.

Sweat still dripped down her back. Without the wind, the heat was almost oppressive. Paige was glad to finally reach Tranquila Inn. She needed a shower, a juice, and a coffee – as in yesterday. Paige didn't care if it made her a coward – she walked the long way around the cottages to avoid running into anyone. Personal growth came in small steps, after all. Ducking into her cottage, she took a long, cold, and invigorating shower before towel-drying her hair, pulling a loose maxi dress over her head, and grabbing her tote bag with her laptop. Heading into the reception hall, she immediately veered away from where Jack huddled with Mariposa, CeCe, and Whit. It was early for CeCe and Whit to be up, Paige thought, but perhaps they were hitting the mimosas for Sunday brunch.

Martin was nowhere to be found in the kitchen, and no food had been left out. That was odd, Paige thought, but dug into the fridge for a carafe of iced coffee he had started brewing regularly for her and a bottle of orange juice. Pouring glasses for herself, Paige then walked into the pantry and retrieved a bag of muffins. She didn't care about carbs today, she thought. All but jamming one blueberry muffin in her mouth, she washed it down with the orange juice before grabbing another and her glass of iced coffee. Knowing there was really no way to avoid the group in the reception hall if she wanted to get to her office, Paige took a steadying breath before leaving the kitchen.

"Watch out, mama!" Luis darted back as Paige almost ran him over at the door.

"Oh, sorry, Luis. I'm distracted this morning. I think I need about a gallon of coffee." Paige said, steadying herself and taking a sip of her coffee.

"We all might. Shit's about to go down."

"Wait, what?"

"You didn't hear?" Luis leaned back, bringing his hand to his chest, his mouth dropping open in surprise. "Well, I suppose that's what you get when you ignore me when I wave you over."

"I thought you were just waving to say hello," Paige grumbled.

"Girl, I *was not*. I was calling you over because we need to get our plan together."

"What in the world are you talking about?" Paige's eyes darted over his shoulder to where the others were huddled around the bar.

"The hurricane?" Luis raised an eyebrow at her.

"What!" Paige almost dropped her coffee.

"I tried to get you, mama, but you ran off like the hounds of hell were at your feet."

"What's happening? Is it going to hit us? What do we do? Where should we hide? We have to do something!" Panic racketed through Paige.

"Whoa. Just calm down. Breathe. We got a little time, yet. Better meet with the group to discuss the action plan."

"But…but…we need to evacuate! We need to pack!"

"Oh, we aren't going anywhere, mama. Don't you know? The airport's closed."

"What? But…how? What if people need to get away? To safety? Are they just going to leave us here to die?" Paige's breathing was coming faster and faster and little spots danced in front of her eyes.

"Okay, that's enough." Luis grabbed her arm and dragged her to a low-slung couch in one of the conversation areas. Grabbing her coffee and her bag, he put them on the table and pushed her onto the couch. "Breathe. Isn't that what you yogis always say? Just breathe."

"What's wrong?" Jack said, having come to the couch, the rest of the group following in his wake. Unable to look at him, Paige bent her head between her knees and drew in long breaths. She'd just taken a long run down an isolated beach and done positive affirmations when a fricking hurricane was bearing down on the island. No wonder it had been so still and all the wind had disappeared. A massive storm had sucked it all up and was about to batter them.

"I think she's having a little panic attack about the hurricane."

"I'm not…" Paige took a few more deep breaths and brought her head up. She refused to look at Jack and instead focused on Luis. "I just needed a moment. Hurricanes are completely out of my depth. I have no idea what to do."

"We'll get an action plan together and we'll alert the guests. Why don't we do that now?" Jack spoke in a soothing tone, but still Paige turned from him. Instead her eyes landed on Mariposa, a strong island woman, and her calmness steadied Paige.

"You can do this." Mariposa's brown eyes held Paige's, and she wondered if the bartender spoke of more than just the hurricane.

"Please. Can someone just tell me what they know?"

"Well, darling, we've been keeping an eye on this one. The weather center has been tracking a tropical depression this week and while we were alerted to it, at the time it seemed to be not much to worry about," Whit said as he took a seat across from Paige. Grateful for anywhere to look but at Jack, Paige nodded for him to continue. "However, overnight it met up with another weather pattern that whipped it quickly into a Cat three. It's bearing down on us directly."

"A Cat three? That sounds bad."

"It's not the best news, no. But better than a Category four or five. Five can be catastrophic. Three is likely going to be a might bit painful." Whit said this as casually as if he was commenting on a new item on the menu for dinner.

"Painful?" Paige asked.

"Well, Category Three hurricanes typically have around one hundred mile per hour winds. It's certainly nothing to be trifled with."

Paige's mouth dropped open and her stomach sank.

"But…what are we going to do? We have to get off this island."

"Not happening," Jack bit out. "As we've mentioned… they've closed the airport. The hurricane should be here by nightfall. All we can do is alert the guests and begin our emergency action plan."

"I don't have a plan. Where's the plan? I was never given a plan." Paige's hands fluttered weakly in front of her as she looked around. At everyone but Jack, of course.

"I've printed them out, gorgeous. We've got a stack at the bar to hand out. It's best if we collect the guests and begin our safety procedures. It's best not to panic, you know, as then the guests will panic. So, if you can't pull yourself together, then I suggest you retire to your cabin until you can," CeCe said, calmly smoothing a crease in her linen pants.

It was CeCe's tone that had Paige snapping out of her panic. It spoke of disapproval and almost...disappointment? It was as though she expected better of Paige. Well, Paige had expected...actually, now that Paige thought about it, she hadn't expected much of CeCe. The woman clearly did whatever she felt like – whenever she felt like. What a blissful life that must be to lead.

"Understood." Paige took one more deep breath and then reached for her coffee. "I'm excellent at following checklists. If you can tell me what I need to do, I'll get on it."

"Time is of the essence. T-minus eight hours before this beast hits," Whit said, studying the phone in his hand.

Why did his words feel like a death sentence?

CHAPTER TWENTY-SIX

Paige didn't know what was causing her more anxiety – the impending storm or the fact that as soon as she'd decided to leave the island the airport had quite literally been closed to her. It was like the Universe was forcing her to stay in one spot and deal with her shit, even though all Paige wanted to do was run away, lick her wounds, and start fresh with all of this behind her. Never say the Universe doesn't have a sense of humor, she thought.

Instead, now she sat grouped with the guests and other employees in the reception hall, while Jack stood in front of them with a clipboard in hand.

"First of all, let me make this very clear. This is an extremely serious situation. In other times, we would have tried to move you inland, but the storm is already making its way up the coast and time is of the essence. Because of this, your safety is our priority. Those of you who want to go to our designated safe house may do so now – otherwise – those who are willing and able to help us prepare, well, we can use all hands on deck. So, who would like to retire to the safe house? Mariposa will explain what to bring with you from your cabins and she will lead that group."

A smattering of people raised their hands. Paige didn't blame them. She wanted to go with Mariposa, too, but knew that Tranquila Inn needed her help.

"No problem. All of you going with Mariposa, please leave now and listen to her instructions. When she tells you to only bring what is on her designated list, she means that. Your bag full of clothes is irrelevant. Medications, first-aid, food, and your phones or laptops are fine. The rest – if it can be replaced easily – it doesn't matter."

With that, Mariposa took her group to the other side of the hall and began to issue instructions.

"Where's the safe house?" Stan asked. He'd stayed behind to help and now looked around curiously at the reception hall. Paige didn't blame him for his question – not much about the hotel looked to be sturdy when a hurricane was bearing down on them.

"We have a concrete garage on the other side of the property. It has only small windows situated high for ventilation. It's the safest spot on the resort."

"Sounds good. What else can we do?" Stan asked.

"I'll be breaking everyone else into teams with clearly designated roles so that nobody overlaps their duties. Our housekeeping and grounds staff will take care of bringing in any furniture that can be potential projectiles. This means sun loungers, beach chairs, umbrellas, coconuts… the works. You all know what to do?" Jack addressed the staff and they all nodded. "I want to remind you that you don't have to work here right now – I can't force you to be here. If you need to go to your families, then do so now." A few people got up and left without another word while others stayed. "Okay, for the rest of you – here is your list."

Turning, Jack met her eyes, and Paige looked quickly away, her stomach roiling from anxiety. Even though she hated what she'd learned, he still looked good. Like, really good. Totally in charge, competent, and calm – his confidence made her want him even more.

Stupid hormones, Paige thought, and blinked down at the sheet in her hand. The sheer amount of tasks listed there seemed daunting.

"Next up, I need a group to go around and board up all the cottage windows, pull down the hurricane shutters for the bar, and duct-tape up any glass windows that can't be boarded up. Volunteers?" Several men raised their hands at that task. Jack nodded to Luis. "Luis will answer your questions with all of that. He knows the grounds inside and out and can tell you where the biggest risks are."

"Gentlemen? Shall we?" With that, Luis disappeared with the group of men, pointing to the windows of the cottages.

"Next up. We need food and medical supplies transported to the safe house. We'll need ice put into coolers and any food that can be eaten easily but needs to be kept cool dropped into those coolers. Grab other non-perishable items that are easy to eat and bag them up. Water is the most important. We have an entire pantry full of water jugs. Those that aren't filled will need to be filled and transported. There's a golf cart out front that can be used to make the trip to the kitchen and back. Paige? Can you do that?"

"Sure, no problem," Paige said automatically.

"Great. Everyone that can help with that, go with Paige. For the rest of you, I have various tasks. We need generators, sandbags, paperwork in pelican cases, gas tanks secured, radios, flashlights, candles and so on. We do have several hurricane kits prepared, but because this is a larger group than we'd usually have here for a storm, we have more to do."

"Paige. The food?" Lily asked and Paige turned, blinking at the group of women who had collected around her.

"Okay. But before we even go to the kitchen, I want each of you to return to your cottages and get everything that is a must for you. That means your medication, your eyeglasses, your phone, phone chargers, and anything that you can't replace. If you have a rain jacket or something to keep you warm, grab that, too. We'll meet at the kitchen in fifteen minutes, but I don't want you to forget anything that is absolutely essential to your well-being. That means heart medication and so-on. Understood?" Paige met the eyes of each member and they all nodded. "Okay, go team. Fifteen minutes."

Paige glanced up as the wind began to pick up, the palm fronds fluttering wildly in the trees.

"And watch for coconuts!"

"Paige." Jack grabbed her arm before she could race off. Turning, she finally met his eyes.

"Are you okay?"

"I'm about as fine as can be with a catastrophe bearing down on my head," Paige bit out.

"About last night…" Jack lowered his voice.

"There's nothing to be said about last night." Paige wrenched her arm from his hand. "Now that I know you're just like Horatio, I can promise you there won't be a repeat."

"What the hell does that mean?" Fury thundered across Jack's face.

"You take advantage of women to get what you want. Whether they pay your salary or you just want to win the little *one-up* war you have going with Horatio. Happy, are you? Did you boast to him this morning that I chose you instead of him? Or were you too busy with your other women?" Paige couldn't bring herself to say CeCe's name. The thought of the two of them together made her stomach turn.

"Have you lost your fucking mind?" Jack started to grip her arm again, but Paige stepped back and out of his reach. "Being with you last night had nothing to do with Horatio. And I resent the fact you think I'm anything like that ego-driven piece of shit."

"Yes, because being called crazy does wonders for women. You men are all the same." Paige looked pointedly to where Whit soothed a distraught Lily. "Whoever strokes your ego enough gets your attention. I'm not interested in being a pawn in your game. Leave me alone – I have to go do my job. While I still have one, that is…" Paige turned from him and raced to her office, but not before she saw the look of hurt cross his face. How could he be hurt? It wasn't like *she* was the one leading a double life.

Annoyed, she ducked under her desk and pulled out a waterproof pelican case and began dumping all the important paperwork into the case. Once she'd finished that, she added her laptop and anything else that she thought the hotel would need copies for insurance claims. Once she was finished, she dragged the case into the reception hall, dropped it by the kitchen door, and raced back to her cabin. Heart pounding, Paige scooped up a backpack and stuffed her birth control pills, a first-aid kit, a few pieces of protective clothing, and her phone charger in the bag. Stopping, she took a quick scan. Her entire life, aside from what was stuffed in the shed behind Jane's house, was in this cottage. In the closet were her favorite dresses, her best yoga clothes, and shoes she'd had for years. It might not be much, but Paige had worked hard for everything she had and it hurt to close the door behind her, knowing she couldn't bring it with her.

As a guest raced by her, Paige shook off her sadness. There was really no time to waste worrying about things she could replace if she had to. Threading her arms through the strap of her backpack, Paige rushed to meet the group that had gathered by the kitchen door.

"Okay. Okay. Did everyone get what they needed from their cabins?"

The group all replied in the affirmative.

"How about two of you take everyone's bags to the garage? There's the golf cart." Paige pointed to the front drive where a golf cart that resembled more of a mini pick-up truck sat, ready for use. "The rest of us will start packing food."

Two women broke off from the group and started

picking up bags, and Paige pulled the rest of the women into the kitchen.

"We need water jugs. Coolers with ice. Easy-to-eat food. Grab all the fruit, the muffins, any granola bars, cereal…that kind of stuff." Paige started opening drawers and digging around. "Here. I've got large trash bags. Dump all the food in these. We don't know how long we'll be in there so take as much as you can."

The women grabbed bags from the box and split up. Paige pulled the folded paper from her pocket and scanned the list.

"Candles. Knives. Can openers. Matches." Paige opened drawers at random and began to add stuff to her bag, her heart racing as sweat trickled down her neck. It felt like they had so much to do and so little time. However, in under an hour the group had assembled a large portion of the kitchen contents and had divided it into bags and coolers as needed. One by one, they carried everything out into the reception hall and Paige's mouth dropped open when she emerged.

Everything was gone.

The bar across the way had steel hurricane proof shutters that had been pulled down and secured, essentially eradicating any chance of liquor bottles becoming flying projectiles. All the bar stools, side tables, chairs and even the couches had been stacked and roped together on one side of the hall. Turning, Paige saw that the beach had been cleared and the cottages all had their shutters secured. A group of people loaded any vehicles they had with supplies in the front drive.

Everyone was quiet.

It was the silence that raised Paige's anxiety more than anything. Aside from the sound of increasing wind and a few grunts from people as they hefted bags into the trucks, the quiet enveloped them like a funeral shroud.

The entire island seemed to have drawn a collective breath, and now they waited.

CHAPTER TWENTY-SEVEN

It was smelly.

That was one thing Paige quickly realized and hadn't been expecting about being in a concrete bunker with a large group of people. Granted, she hadn't given much thought to what it would be like stuck in a concrete bunker with fifty people before, but nevertheless, here she was. It made sense, though. They had all just run around for hours securing the property, and the heat certainly hadn't abated. Paige couldn't have been the only one dripping in sweat as they worked. Now she could say with absolute certainty that being stuck in a lightly ventilated area with a group of sweaty people was…stinky.

Someone had taken it upon themselves to load the lounge cushions into the truck and had laid them across the floor of the garage, which helped to make the space significantly more comfortable. Grateful for small comforts, Paige shifted on her cushion, ignoring the twinges of soreness from her night with Jack. Paige had stationed herself in one corner, a bit away from the main group, as she just didn't have it in her to do any more customer-servicing. Luckily, Horatio was avoiding her and had gathered a group of his "followers" in another corner to lead them in some sort of anti-hurricane prayer or meditation. She wasn't really sure and honestly didn't care. After Horatio had spent a good portion of an hour having a melt-down about what he was allowed to bring with him from his cabin, Paige had handed him off to CeCe who had dealt with his antics masterfully. As far as Paige was concerned, Horatio could do without his comfort tunics or his gong. In fact, he could just go stay in his cabin if that was what he needed. Feeling surly, Paige wrapped her arms around her legs and rested her head on her knees. Closing her eyes for the first time in hours, she allowed herself to rest as her brain tried to take stock of everything that had happened that day.

"Are you okay?"

Paige opened her eyes when she felt the cushion move next to her and saw Mariposa, accompanied by a pretty little girl.

"I am. Is this your daughter?"

"Yes, this is Estrella. Can you say hi to Paige?"

"Hola." The child smiled shyly up at her and clung to her mother's side.

"Do you want to color? There's crayons and paper in your backpack."

Estrella nodded and scurried over to where a pink backpack sat on the floor. Her hair was pulled back in one long braid and she wore simple denim shorts and a striped pink t-shirt.

"When did you leave to get her? I didn't realize you had gone."

"Jack said my family could come here. Our house…it is not secure. And it is just my mother and my grandparents." Mariposa nodded to a group huddled across the room. "I feel safer with them here."

"Good, I'm glad you were able to get them here in time. Is this what it's always like?" Paige wondered, leaning back against the gritty concrete wall.

"It depends." Mariposa shrugged one shoulder. "Sometimes it is not such a rush, and we have more notice. Or if the category of the storm is meant to be smaller. Storms, well, they are moody. They change course when they feel like it. They get stronger. Weaker. It's God's will."

"And now we wait."

"Yes, that is often the hardest part. The waiting. You don't know how long you are stuck inside. You don't know what damage will be done. If people will get hurt. If your house will be there when you get back."

"How are you so calm? This is a horrible way to live. This…not knowing." Paige looked at her in confusion. "And this happens every year?"

"Not every year. And not always so bad. Every country has natural disasters. Most people here? They can't afford to leave and start a new life elsewhere. So they make the best of what they have. It's not a bad life, Paige. But, like with anything, you have to accept the good with the bad."

Despite herself, Paige's eyes landed on where Jack crouched by a group of people, speaking softly to them.

"Sometimes the bad outweighs the good."

Mariposa followed her gaze.

"It depends. What are you willing to put up with in your life? Nothing is perfect. No matter how much you want it to be. Even yourself."

"I thought we were talking about the island."

"Were we?" Mariposa's eyes crinkled at the corner as she smiled at Paige. "You've been cold to him today."

"Yes. Well…" Paige plucked a piece of a leaf off of her pants. She'd taken the time to change from her dress into leggings and a t-shirt, thinking she'd be more comfortable if they had to evacuate at some point. "It's been a difficult day."

"Is that all? What's changed between you two? I thought…for a while there…" Mariposa raised her eyebrows.

"I thought for a while there that you two…" Paige deftly changed the subject.

"Us?" Mariposa threw her head back and laughed. Paige noticed that more than one man looked up at her laugh. "No, no, never. He's like a brother to me. Family. That is all."

"He seems pretty familiar with you. With a lot of people here." Paige pushed her lip out sullenly.

"Talk to him before you judge him. Everybody has their own story. Myself included."

"There's nothing to be said. I already know everything I need to know," Paige said, a stubborn note in her voice.

"Ah, Estrella," Mariposa raised her voice to her daughter. "What do I tell you about people who think they know everything?"

"That they really know nothing at all." Estrella's tiny voice was like a little hammer strike to Paige's gut.

"A closed mind is an empty one." Mariposa tapped her forehead with a finger. Then she cocked her head, listening. "Shh. Listen. It gets worse."

A rush of fear washed through Paige and she pulled her legs more tightly to her chest. There was nothing else she could do now. She had no control over the situation and there was nowhere to run. All they could do was wait as the storm bore down on them.

"It's coming."

A hush fell over the group, and a few whimpers sounded. People drew closer to each other as darkness fell outside. The winds had been picking up for hours, but now it sounded like a freight train hurtling toward them. Panic seized Paige's stomach and she buried her face in her legs, with no idea what to expect. A loud crash sounded outside, and someone wailed from the other side of the room. Paige closed her eyes, not wanting to see, wanting to be anywhere else than where she was.

"Are you okay?" It was Jack's voice, as he went around from person to person. She heard him stop by her, but he didn't speak. Instead, he moved on to the next person and her heart cracked even more. Jack's words carried as he went around the room, checking on each person, making sure they had water or other needs tended to.

"When will it be over?" Paige asked, turning to look at Mariposa. The sound outside was incredible, like a lion roaring its rage, and the roof trembled as rain lashed it in sheets.

"Oh, hours. It could be hours and hours. It depends how fast the storm moves. Some of them are real quick.

Others hunker in and hang out for a while. Those are the really bad ones. If it goes on for days, you can lose everything."

"Days…" Paige's mouth dropped open. "You can't be serious."

"I am."

The wind did not abate, and nobody slept. Instead they stayed huddled together and doled out food and water as necessary. The complaints had started about going to the restroom. Paige herself desperately needed to pee, and didn't know what she would do if this went on much longer.

Jack stood at the back of the garage. They'd turned on some solar charged lamps, and she could see the tension etched in his handsome face. He moved across the large garage space and stopped by a door in the back.

"I understand we all need to use the bathroom. I'm going to check if the next room behind this door is structurally safe and if so, this will be an option. It…well, it won't be pretty, but it's better than the alternative."

With that, Jack ducked through the door, closing it quickly behind him.

"I get to go first." Horatio stood and made his way to the door.

"Why do you get to go first?" A woman demanded. "There's children here."

"Because I'm a paying guest and the leader of this group," Horatio shot back, and Paige's eyebrows went almost to her hairline at his response.

"Don't you think as the leader of a business that exists solely because people pay you to help them on their path to better health, it makes sense to let others see to their needs first?" Paige blinked for a moment when the whole room turned to look at her. Oops. She'd said that out loud.

"Oh, Miss High and Mighty over there thinks she knows what is best? Is that why you invited me to your cabin last night? You were worried for our guests' health?"

Paige's mouth dropped open.

"What? That doesn't even make sense! And I didn't invite you to my cabin. You shoved your way in."

"Nice try, Paige. We all know you've been dying to redeem your position at Yoga Soulone. You'd do anything to be in a position of power, wouldn't you? Isn't that why you slept with Jack as well?"

"You dirty piece of…" Paige was on her feet in a flash and Mariposa grabbed her arm, pulling her back.

"Don't let him get to you, mama. He's nothing. Dirt." Mariposa hissed in her ear.

"You are a cheat," Paige bit out, raising her chin at Horatio. "A cheat, a liar, and a fake. You don't deserve these good people to be your clients. You take their hard-earned money and make a joke of them."

The mood of the room shifted as everyone's eyes bounced between Paige and Horatio.

"I only take what people are willing to give. We all have to give something on our path to lightness." Horatio, knowing he had an audience, put a benevolent expression on his face.

"Is that why you take free handouts? And use people? Like the guesthouse Shirley allows you to live in for free?" A gasp went through the room. "Or the free clothes you get from Lily's store? Or what about the free spray-tan and

Botox services from Nadia's medical spa? I bet they don't know that she comps you for them."

"You give him free Botox?" Lily whirled on Nadia. "You made me pay for mine, and I make less money than the both of you."

"You're staying rent-free at his pool house. You can afford it!" Nadia shouted back. In moments, the guests turned on each other, the tension having ratcheted so high that everyone exploded.

"And. You. Keep. Flirting. With. The. Bartender!" Stan's wife smacked him over the head repeatedly with her purse.

"Yoo-hoo! Yooooo-hooo!" CeCe forged her way into the middle of the room, clapping her hands together. Everyone silenced and looked at her. "I've got just the thing to settle all this. Who wants a rum punch?"

Paige opened her mouth to stop CeCe from adding alcohol to this powder keg of a garage, but there was no stopping this crowd. Everyone clamored to the corner where Whit stood by a huge jug and doled out plastic cups of punch.

"When in doubt..." Mariposa shook her head at the group.

"What's going on here?" Jack popped his head back in the door and looked at the crowd around CeCe.

"Why, it's cocktail hour, darling," CeCe laughed.

"It's eight in the morning."

"A perfect time for a drink, don't you think?"

Seeing as the damage was already done, Jack just sighed and pinched his nose.

"Listen up everyone. The bathroom is open. You need

to go one at a time and walk along the back left concrete wall. I've put a little bench for the ladies. There are a couple large rolls of paper towel. There's...well. It's going to be gross, I guess. But it's the only option we have. Is that okay by everyone?"

"Of course." Horatio ducked through the door before anyone else could and the group glared after him.

"I hope he gets hit with a coconut," Lily griped.

"Oh, shut up, Lily," Nadia said.

By the time noon had come, the group was suitably numbed with alcohol, except for Paige, Jack, and Mariposa. Finally seeing her chance to use the bathroom, she crept across half-passed out people and made her way to the door. Opening it, Paige shivered at the gusts of wind that rattled the building. At times through the night, it had felt like the very roof over their heads would be ripped off. But now, it seemed to have grown a bit quieter. Hopeful that they wouldn't be stuck in here too much longer, Paige awkwardly crouched in a corner and went potty, pinching her nose closed against the stench in the room. She was just finishing up when the door opened.

"CeCe?" Paige asked, caught – quite literally – with her pants down.

CeCe smiled tremulously at her, and then darted across the room and out the door to the outside.

"CeCe!" Paige shouted, and then all but tripped over herself trying to pull her pants up and not fall face first into the waste around her. Rushing to the door, she looked out but couldn't see a thing through the rain that still careened down in sheets. The storm had lessened, but not abated.

And CeCe was gone.

Turning, she ran to the garage door and threw it open. "Jack!"

Jack jumped up from his corner, snatched up his rain jacket, and raced to her.

"CeCe ran out."

"God damn it." Jack was gone before Paige could do anything. Without another thought, she followed him into the storm.

CHAPTER TWENTY-EIGHT

Perhaps not her brightest choice, Paige immediately realized, as the wind threatened to knock her over. Rain whipped into her face, and she dashed forward, trying to keep the flash of red from Jack's rain slicker in her sights. She stumbled as another gust of wind bore down on her.

This was where her weight and her muscles came into play, Paige told herself as she forged forward. A little whisp of nothing like Lily would have been thrown into a side of a building by now. But Paige was strong, and even though the storm continued on, it wasn't nearly as terrifying as it had been hours before. She wondered if they were moving into the eye of the storm or if the storm was actually almost over.

Paige reached the reception hall and was shocked to see the destruction. Even though the chairs had been all tied together, they'd been flung across the hall and lay in haphazard piles. The door covering the bar had held, but palm trees and debris littered the wide open air hall. A flash of red caught Paige's eyes, and she saw Jack running between the cabins, ducking his head into doors. Following him, she called out.

"Jack!"

Jack turned as Paige raced to him. Fury ripped across his face.

"What are you doing here? Go back!" Jack shouted, pointing back the way she'd come.

"I can't. I have to help you." Paige had to scream over the roar of the wind.

"I can't worry about you, too." Jack surprised her by taking her shoulders and giving her a small shove.

"You can't make me."

"I can't pay attention to you and find her, too. It's too risky!"

"I'm not leaving you by yourself."

"I can handle this on my own."

"Stop arguing with me. We don't have much time." Paige wiped the rain from her face, her chest heaving as she stared him down.

"You have to go," Jack tried once more.

"You're not alone, Jack."

"It's better if I am."

Paige didn't know what they were talking about anymore, and she didn't care when movement behind Jack caught her eye.

"There!" Paige shouted, pointing to the water.

"Damn it!" Jack turned and grabbing Paige's arm, he hauled her with him. Together they raced to the beach, bending at the waist as the wind picked up. Paige skidded to a stop, gasping at the sight that greeted her.

There, CeCe waded in the cove, water to her waist, her arms held to the sky. She laughed, and laughed, twirling in madness, as the winds tore at her hair and waves battered her small body. More than once, she was tossed about, only to bob to the surface once more and shout to the sky. She danced and danced as the storm raged around her.

"Mom!" Jack screamed, terror lancing his voice.

Paige gasped as everything suddenly became crystal clear to her. The familiarity. The whispered "I love you." The constant annoyance that Jack held for CeCe. She watched, helpless as Jack waded into the sea after his mother.

If she went after them, she'd only hamper his progress.

CeCe disappeared once more as another large wave crashed over her. The sea was like nothing Paige had ever seen before. Usually the waves would come in easy sets of three, careening gently into the shore. But not now. There was barely any time between when one wave hit and another would crash right behind it. The sea had turned an ugly mottled gray color, strewn with debris, with sand churned into its waters. Gone was the clear blue oasis of calm waters, and instead a dark beast rampaged their depths. Paige held her breath, not knowing what to do as Jack surfaced, and dove once more beneath a large wave that shattered over his head.

Tears streamed down her cheeks as Paige realized she might lose them both. Whirling, she looked for anything she could find to help. Spying the dock, Paige pushed her way against the wind across the beach, her feet digging into the sand, her legs like lead. When she reached the dock, she found the rope still tied to the bracket, though the dinghy was long gone. Untying the rope, Paige turned and flew back across the beach, the wind helping her at her back this time, and skidded to a stop where she'd last seen Jack.

"Jack!" Paige shouted, waving when he surfaced with CeCe in his arms. Wading into the water, Paige brandished the rope above her head. "Jack!"

He turned, bowing against another wave that slammed into his back, his mother cradled in his arms. His eyes, ravaged with fear, met hers.

"Rope!" Paige shouted and he nodded.

Paige wound it up and threw it with all her might, and a gust of wind helped it reach them. Maybe the universe did have her back sometimes, Paige thought, as she dropped to her knees at the waterline and wrapped the other end of the rope around her body. The rope went tight, and Paige bowed over, closing her eyes against the sand and the saltwater that buffeted her face, and she held on with all her might as Jack pulled himself closer to shore. Tears streamed down her face and Paige sobbed…for CeCe…for Jack…for all of them as they waited for the storm to finish unleashing her fury.

When the rope went loose, Paige looked up to see Jack on his knees in the sand, cradling CeCe to his chest. Blood dripped from her forehead, her arms, and even on her legs. Jack had a particularly nasty scrape oozing blood on his forehead. Paige couldn't bring herself to stand. She didn't know if she could handle it if CeCe was gone. When CeCe finally moved, throwing her head back and laughing, before reaching up to pat Jack's face, Paige choked out a sob. She was alive.

And Jack was destroyed.

Paige could see it in his eyes when he stood, looking down at his mother with love, but also with anger. She'd put herself in danger. Him in danger. And when Jack looked at Paige, she realized he cared about her, too.

"Are you okay?" Jack asked, his voice gruff, as CeCe giggled in his arms like a madwoman.

"I'm fine. Are you...is she?"

"Wasn't that most marvelous fun, darling? Oh, I do love a good storm!" CeCe crowed, oblivious to the wounds that marred her fragile body.

"She's fine," Jack bit out. "Let's go. I think the worst is over."

"Jack..." Paige wanted to apologize to him...to explain why she'd turned her back on him earlier that day. But when he turned and just shook his head at her, she left it.

He was right. The storm had passed.

But now a new one seethed inside her.

CHAPTER TWENTY-NINE

"I'm sorry for the things I said when we were stuck in the middle of a hurricane."

Paige rolled her eyes as Lily and Nadia embraced, back to being best friends or lovers...or whatever they were. At this point, she no longer cared. It was hard to care about much other than the fact that they'd all managed to survive, though Tranquila Inn had suffered its fair share of damage.

The storm had passed, winging out over the ocean and leaving Poco Poco Island in its wake, gasping and battered. They wouldn't know the extent of the damage to the island until their power was restored, but based on the little snippets of radio reports they were able to receive, it sounded like Poco Poco Island had been bruised, but was certainly not broken. The good news was that the airport would be cleaned of debris and would be operational by the following day. Paige couldn't get this group away from her soon enough.

The guests had gathered in the reception hall, and they

all looked shell-shocked as they took stock of the damage to the inn. Tranquila had been lucky – what could have been total obliteration had ended up largely being surface damage that could be cleaned or patched up. What had looked like total chaos in the early morning hours of the storm to Paige was mainly debris and brush that had been tossed about in the winds.

"Since we've got nothing else to do – I say we help put this place back to rights. What do you think?" Stan spoke up, looking around at the others. Notably, Horatio remained silent and hovered at the back of the group – no longer sure of his place. Paige almost felt sorry for him. The guests quickly agreed and Paige was surprised to see Stan call Luis over, and they all listened quietly as the gardener gave instructions on where to pile up the debris.

"I hardly think picking up trash is part of our obligation as guests," Horatio said at her ear. Had Paige thought she might feel sorry for him? That quickly vanished as she turned to look at Horatio with disgust.

"It's not part of your obligation as guests. But it's what a decent human being would do." Paige glared at him, hands on hips, and he hunched his shoulders.

"I'm just saying…"

"Don't you think that's your problem? You're always just saying *this* and just saying *that*. Have you ever considered, just for once, shutting the fuck up? People might respect you a lot more if you stopped offering your opinion on every damn thing." Horatio's eyes rounded at her words, and he had the gall to look like she'd slapped him.

"Anger comes from…" Horatio began and Paige raised her hand.

"Yeah, yeah, I know. And I don't care. If you can't keep your mouth shut and if you can't help...then I suggest you make yourself scarce. Nobody likes a lazy freeloader." Not bothering to wait to hear if he had anything else to say, Paige moved forward to join the group and listen to Luis's instructions. Once she'd been assigned the task of clearing trash from the beach, Paige disappeared without a word.

She was talked out, Paige realized. Talked out, burnt out, and she kept vacillating between wanting to cry or laugh hysterically. Her entire body was one large exposed nerve ending and the slightest touch could send her over the edge.

Jack had disappeared with CeCe immediately after he'd rescued her on the beach that morning. When Paige had asked Whit about their condition, he'd merely informed her both were well and had gently pushed her back to the group. It was as though the wagons had circled, protecting their little family unit, and Paige was now an outsider. Stung, Paige had retreated – her mind whirling.

Now, as she shoved trash into a garbage bag, Paige wondered if Jack could forgive her. He was clearly furious with her – not only because she'd rejected and accused him, but because she'd also seen him at his most vulnerable. CeCe needed help. And Whit...well...he seemed to do exactly what he wanted. The hotel was a mess and, if Paige was honest with herself, so was she. What had she been thinking, letting herself care for Jack? She'd promised herself she was going to make better choices this time around and yet here she was...picking up food cartons and plastic bags on the beach and wondering how the hell she'd landed on tiny Poco Poco Island.

Jack needed her.

Paige shivered as the thought raced through her. His face in the storm…it was like all his carefully crafted walls had been ripped down and instead a vulnerable little boy who cried out for love had peered out at her. He'd spent his whole life cleaning up CeCe's messes and he was used to being alone – in fact he thrived on his ability to take care of himself. It was almost as though he'd expected Paige's rejection because everybody in his life always failed him.

The problem was Paige didn't know what to do about it. She didn't know if she had it in her to stay, or if she would even be invited to continue to work at Tranquila Inn. The future of the hotel remained uncertain, as far as Paige knew, because there was no way they could operate with CeCe at its head. She was a liability and she'd proven that when she'd almost gotten both her and Jack killed.

Tears pricked Paige's eyes as she recalled CeCe dancing in the waves, innocent as a child and mad as a hatter. Her appeal lay in her charm and her threat in her addiction. It would be a tough road to navigate, and Paige felt like an outsider looking in – wanting to help but not knowing what the right answer was.

When her foot squelched into something wet and mushy, Paige closed her eyes briefly before looking down at the diaper she'd just stepped in. If this wasn't a metaphor for her life, Paige wasn't sure what was. Sighing, she gingerly picked up the diaper, tossed it in the bag, and went to rinse her feet in the ocean. Standing in the calm waters, Paige took a moment to breathe.

To just breathe.

Inhale…exhale. The saltwater felt soothing on her feet, and the sand massaged her toes. The ocean was calm today, as though the chaos of last night was a mistake, and it begged her forgiveness as it washed away the dirt that clung to her. "Everything will be fine," the ocean seemed to whisper. "Life will always be messy. But oh, it's so incredibly beautiful, too."

Paige found her center, and reminded herself that not everything she'd experienced was bad. She'd made friends, learned new skills, and had forged new paths for herself. While she wasn't particularly happy with how she'd been taken for a ride by Horatio, she'd also learned a valuable lesson about herself.

That even she could weather the storm. She may bend in the force of the wind, but she did not break.

Hours later, Paige had filled sixteen trash bags and her muscles ached – not to mention she was starving. She'd successfully avoided interacting with people and now wove her way to her cabin to take stock of any damage to her personal belongings. Finding everything intact made her happier than Paige had thought it would, so she supposed she had some connection to her material posses-sions after all. And that was okay, Paige told herself, shoving Horatio's guru-speak about the evil of material possessions from her mind. So what if she liked her stuff? She'd worked hard for it.

Taking a long shower – and not even caring that there was no hot water – Paige scrubbed every inch of herself as though she could rub away the mess of the last thirty-six hours. When finished, she toweled off, pulled a loose maxi dress over her head and went in search of food.

"Martin!" Paige exclaimed, surprised to see the chef darting around the kitchen, an annoyed expression on his face. "I was worried about you."

"Me? I'm just fine, honey. I had to go be with my family. But the storm barely touched us. We are good."

"I'm glad to hear it. How has the rest of the island fared?" Paige leaned her hip against the stainless-steel table and watched as the chef slammed a drawer closed.

"It's not the worst one we've had. Some damage, but nothing that can't be built back up. I'd say we are damn lucky." The chef slammed another drawer.

"Are you upset about something?" Paige tilted her head at him in question and the chef whirled on her.

"Yes! Everyone was in my kitchen. Nothing is in the right place. I'll have to reorganize everything. I can't find anything. What did you guys do here? Get drunk and empty my shelves?"

Wisely, Paige didn't answer and pressed her lips together in a thin seam to avoid laughing. It would only make him angrier, and she genuinely liked the chef.

"I can help you put it back together." Paige walked over to where he stood and smiled up at him. "I'm really glad you're safe, Martin."

"Ah, well, it's fine. I'll get it put back together. It's not the first hurricane I've cleaned up after." Martin shrugged and then shot a glare over Paige's head. Turning, she saw Horatio hovering in the doorway.

"Um, I was just wondering when dinner would be served?"

"Dinner will be served when I damn well feel like serving it. Do you have any other questions?" Martin's tone was lethal, and Horatio opened his mouth and then ducked out of the kitchen, seemingly thinking better of pushing the chef. Frankly, for him that was hugely perceptive, Paige thought.

"I hope you've let that idiot go by now." Martin shook his head as he pulled out several mixing bowls and put them on the table. "He's not right for you, my beauty."

"I...yes, I've let him go. Well, he let me go, I guess."

"Did he? You still seemed bothered by him when he arrived."

Speaking of perceptive, Paige thought, and pushed back the annoyance that wanted to rear its ugly head. That was just her hangry talking, and her stomach growled loudly. Muttering, Martin ducked his head in the pantry and returned with a basket of muffins. "Eat this until I can feed you properly."

"Thank you," Paige said. She grabbed a muffin and considered Martin's words. "I still get frustrated by Horatio, if that's what you're asking. But I no longer want a relationship with him or have romantic feelings for him."

"It's not your path anymore. So there shouldn't even be frustration."

"How so?" Paige didn't even care that she spoke over a mouthful of blueberry deliciousness.

"It's like this, honey." Martin cracked eggs into a bowl. "You and Horatio are approaching a big mountain together. You're on a hike...it's maybe not the best hike, but somewhat scenic and then you come to a split in the road. You want to go up, you get it? Because at the top of that trail… well, the views are world-class. The best. But Horatio, well, he wants to take the easier path. The one along the cliffs."

"Right." Paige had no idea what he was talking about, but nodded vigorously when the chef shot her a look.

"Horatio likes the easy path. He's convinced it will be better and the view just as pretty. But what he doesn't know is that the path is washed out and there are loads of boulders and awful prickly bushes to get through to see his views. So he takes that route. But you decide to go up. To take the higher road."

"Okay…" Paige figured this was a lesson on being the better person. Which she totally understood, but had to admit it was pretty annoying when you always had to be the person to take the high road.

"Your choice was the better choice all along. The climb isn't without its share of problems, but nothing like the path Horatio chose. And once you get to the top and you see the stunning views…you know what?"

"What?"

"You're not worried about Horatio anymore. He's on his path. That was *his* choice. And you are on yours. They are no longer shared. He'll encounter problem after problem on the road he takes. And that's just fine. That's *his* path. Not yours. You, my beauty, get to go your own way and the only thing *you* have to think about is where you place your next step."

"Because we're on different paths."

"Precisely. You can't control his path or his choices

anymore. You can only focus on your own. If he chooses to climb a boulder and slips and falls over a cliff edge to a gory death, well…"

"That's on him."

"Exactly."

"And it's not my fault."

"No, love. The police wouldn't find his body and see you at the top of the mountain and say you pushed him. You'd only get dragged into it if you were on the same trail as him."

Paige realized it was his convoluted way of saying that each person was responsible for their own destiny, but for some reason…it helped. A lightness that she hadn't felt in years filled her and Paige beamed at Martin.

"Has anyone ever told you how wise you are?"

"Of course, honey." Martin looked at her like she was crazy. "Don't you know chefs always have the best advice?"

"You're right. Thank you." Paige impulsively pressed a kiss to his cheek before wandering to the door.

"Tell the guests food will be on within the hour."

"You're a god among men, Martin."

"Don't I know it." His laughter followed her out the door as Paige crossed the reception hall to the group gathered in front of the bar. By her estimation, the rum punch had already been flowing.

"Hey, Paige." Lily and Nadia broke off and approached her. Paige's shoulders tensed as she studied the two willowy beauties.

"Yes?"

"We're sorry about…you know…"

"Sleeping with my boyfriend?" Paige supplied cheerfully.

"Right, that. We should've known you weren't aware of what was going on." Lily nudged Nadia who rolled her eyes.

"Yes, we're sorry. We were both stupid. Horatio's not that hot anyway."

"No, he's not. I think I like a more distinguished gentleman, anyway," Lily said.

Paige looked between the two of them as they began to bicker about what kind of man made a better lover, and realizing her participation was not required, she turned to leave.

"Hey, Paige. Want a rum punch?" Stan asked, gesturing with a drink. Behind him, Mariposa shot her a soft smile.

"No, I'm good."

"Hey, listen. We're going to miss you at Yoga Soulone. You really helped run a tight ship there. But…if I were you…" Stan looked around at the reception hall and back to Paige. "I'd stay right here. You're better than Horatio and his yoga studio. I think you'll do great things here."

If she even still had a job, Paige echoed silently in her head. Instead, she smiled her thanks at Stan. The noise level of the group ratcheted up as Whit joined the party, and everyone asked after CeCe. Not able to stand whatever explanation Whit would give, Paige left the reception hall and headed for the water.

Which was where Jack found her.

CHAPTER THIRTY

"She's your mom. Not your lover." Paige wrapped her arms around her knees and leaned back against the lounge chair she'd dragged by the water. Jack dropped down at the end of the chair and turned to look at her. His face was expressionless in the moonlight, but his eyes were soft with...was it pain? Or confusion?

"That's why you froze me out?"

"I..." Paige shrugged one shoulder and propped her chin on her knees. "It was early in the morning after we'd just been together. You'd left without a word. And I saw you come out of CeCe's room. You didn't have a shirt on, and she wrapped her arms around you and said she loved you."

"So you just thought that low of me? That I would flit from one woman to the next? With not a care in the world?" Jack looked hugely offended as he leaned back, anger rippling across his handsome face.

"I guess...I guess I don't know." A sliver of embarrassment worked through Paige's gut. "It's what I'm used to."

"Ah. That's insulting. You're holding me to Horatio's standards. Or lowering me, I should say." Jack shook his head and swore softly.

"I...I haven't known you that long. And it's what I've experienced."

"So you just assume every guy will treat you like dirt just because one did?"

"It's good to be cautious." Paige raised her chin at him.

"Cautious would be not sleeping with your boss then."

"Ouch," Paige said, blowing out a breath as his words hit deep.

"Well? I'm not wrong. If you wanted to be cautious and take it slow and get to know someone better before making a mistake again, then you shouldn't have slept with me. You had a say in the decision, too. I didn't force you."

"No, you didn't." Paige held up a hand when Jack wanted to go on. "Just...give me a second."

"Fine."

Paige took a few deep gulps of the salty night air and thought about his words. He wasn't wrong. If she was going to use being more cautious as her excuse, then she absolutely shouldn't have slept with him. She wanted to because...well, she *liked* Jack. *Really* liked him. And he was nothing like Horatio. With everything she'd learned over the weeks working with him every day, Paige knew that Jack was reliable, honorable, and deeply committed to any projects that he put his mind to.

"I owe you an apology," Paige began and held up her hand again when Jack would speak. "No, just let me. You're absolutely right. As much as looking in the mirror isn't exactly fun sometimes…you *are* right. If I wasn't sure about my choice to sleep with you or if I thought you were even remotely capable of being that type of guy, I shouldn't have had sex with you. It was a kneejerk reaction to being hurt by someone so recently. And once the hurricane swept in, well, I didn't really have much time to examine my reaction or my thoughts more deeply."

"You could have just asked me right away, Paige. Instead of treating me like I was some revenge-shag against Horatio or like I was in some battle to one-up him or something." Jack's tone was soft, but it was laced with hurt. Paige blinked at the tears that threatened.

"I wasn't…I didn't!" Paige blinked at him and took a moment. "Okay. I can see why you'd think that. You're right. I should've asked you. I am sorry. I convicted you without a proper investigation. That was wrong. Can you forgive me?"

"I…yes, I can. But only if you'll listen to what I have to say. Because…I really like you, Paige. I care about you. And I want you to stay on at Tranquila. If you want to?"

Now the tears did blur her vision as a mess of emotions knotted in her stomach.

"I…"

"Don't answer that yet. Just…hear me out."

"Okay." Paige blew out a shaky breath and wiped the back of her hands against her cheeks to swipe at the tears.

"Yes, CeCe is my mother. A mother I love very much but who is also a burden to me." Jack scrubbed a hand over his face.

"Is Whit…?"

"Whit is not my father. We don't know my father as I

am a product of one of my dear mother's indiscretions. It's…well, what you see is what you get with CeCe. She's always struggled with alcohol. And every few years, she picks up and moves someplace new. She promises things will be different this time. It's a new location, a new project, and a new life. Often, for a while it is. But it usually falls apart. I do my best to come pull the pieces together, but it's getting tiring."

Paige's heart broke for the poor little boy who just wanted his mother to be happy and healthy.

"Whit…he seems to…" Paige tried to think about how to phrase her next words without calling Jack's stepdad a man-whore.

"Yes. I struggle with Whit's choices. As well as my mother's. The thing is – it works for them. They bicker all the time. But they also seem to love each other as fiercely as they despise each other. I can't say it's a healthy relationship, but it works for them. They are well aware of the other's actions and choices. They know each other's faults. They know how to make each other angry and they know how to make each other happy. But the thing is? For all of Whit's faults, and trust me, I can count many – he sticks. He always sticks with my mom. He takes care of her. He provides for her. He allows her to follow her heart and find joy and fun in the middle of her problems. As much as I want to judge him, I can't."

"How often do you come running to patch things up?" Paige asked quietly.

"Every few years. This time their little project of Tranquila Inn fell right in my wheelhouse, and trust me – it doesn't always. Like the time they decided they wanted to own a monster truck rally racetrack."

"Excuse me…a what?" Paige's mouth dropped open.

"CeCe thought it would be grand fun. And it was, until one of the trucks smashed a few cars that were in the parking lot and not on the track."

"Ooof." Paige's mind whirled as she tried to place the eminently fastidious and upper crust CeCe and Whit in the stands at a monster truck rally.

"Ooof, is right."

"Do you think she chose Tranquila because she knew you'd come and help her?"

"I'm not sure." Jack leaned back and looked to the stars. "At the very least, I was actually happy to come help. I like tackling projects like this, and I really want Tranquila to be a success. I like the island. I like the people. I'm just…"

"Worried CeCe and Whit will blow it all up for you?" Paige asked, remembering how the locals had laughed about Tranquila Inn upon her arrival.

"Basically, yeah. It's…it's kind of a mess."

"Has…has CeCe ever tried treatment?" Paige knew she was picking her way through a minefield.

"Not once. Not a single time." Jack sighed and pinched his nose. "I think the day she does is the day I know I can relax for once."

"You've taken so much on yourself, Jack."

"She's my mother. I love her. What else can I do?" Jack shrugged her words off. Love flooded through Paige as she looked at this handsome, honorable, and inscrutable man sitting at her feet. How could she ever have thought he'd flit from one woman to the next? This was a man who, for the rest of his life, would do everything he could to take care of his mother – and not out of duty. But because of love.

And Paige loved him for it, she realized. She gasped as the realization rocketed through her. Was it possible to love someone this quickly? She pressed a hand to her stomach and took shallow breaths as she tried to wrap her head around the feelings that raced through her. This was definitely more than just liking someone, that was for sure.

"I think you've got a very good heart," Paige finally managed to say, realizing that the lull in the conversation had drawn out. "Have you ever considered letting her handle her own messes for once?"

"I have. But I can't bring myself to let her flounder for long." Jack, the perpetual parent to his mother, Paige thought.

"Who is going to help you clean up yours though?" Paige wondered.

"I can clean up my own messes. I'm not sick. She is."

"I think you're a really great person, Jack." Paige's tone was soft as she felt her way through the conversation, wanting to be careful with her words.

"But you're still going to go." Jack nodded his head once, turning to look out at where the moonlight reflected a path across the dark water. "I can hear it in your voice."

"No, I…" Paige scooted forward on the chair until she could wrap her legs and arms around Jack. With a tug, she pulled him so that he leaned into her and hugged him. Together, they stayed there for a while in silence and looked out across the water.

"I will understand if you need to go," Jack finally said.

"I don't know what I'm going to do yet." Paige held tight when Jack would have pulled away. "I have a lot of confused feelings right now. And I may need a little time to sort through them."

"I feel like if you know…you know."

"Maybe. Maybe not. I've never ridden out a hurricane before. I'm on no sleep and it's been a hell of a long thirty-six hours. I want to take care with my feelings, Jack. I want to take care with yours as well. I'm…well, I'm worried."

"Worried about what?" Jack asked.

That I just might love you already, Paige thought.

"Well, I just kind of did this. I moved in with my boss. I ran a business with him. Am I just recreating my old life because it's what I know? It's what I'm comfortable with? I think I need to have a really good think about all this so when I do make a decision, it's the right one."

"You scared, Paige?" Jack's words were a challenge.

"Oh yeah, I'm petrified," Paige admitted. But not because of the chance she was recreating her old life. Oh no, it was because she was worried that Jack wouldn't love her back.

"It's okay to be scared. I get frightened all the time. But I get up each day and put one foot in front of the other. You can't run away from your life."

"Some would argue that's exactly what I did by coming here."

"Maybe you didn't run away. Maybe you ran toward your life. Did you ever consider that?"

And maybe he was right.

Paige reached up and ran a hand down Jack's face, turning him to face her so that she could claim his lips in a kiss. It was the kiss of all kisses, her angst, her uncertainty, her love all pouring into it. Standing up, she held out her hand to him.

CHAPTER THIRTY-ONE

This time was different and they both knew it. Jack's eyes held hers as he closed the door to her cottage behind him. The click of the lock sent a shiver of anticipation through her. She wished she'd put on something... Paige glanced down at her loose maxi dress. She hadn't bothered with a bra and she couldn't be certain her underwear wasn't a nice serviceable white pair. Not precisely the most seductive of choices.

"I'm a mess," Paige said, a wry smile on her face.

"I think you're the prettiest woman I've ever seen." Jack's words stopped her train of thought and she glanced up at him with surprise.

"You do?"

"Oh yeah." Jack stepped forward and ran his thumb across her bottom lip, sending tendrils of heat through her core. "You're a contrast of sharp edges and softness. Like a knife coated in maple syrup. You swipe at me one moment and the next you're all big eyes and soft smiles. I knew it when I first saw you – I told you that. I loved that you were an absolute mess. Sweaty. Annoyed. And ready to challenge anyone who got in your way. I liked the fire in your eyes."

"I'll admit…" Paige licked her lips as Jack's hands came to her waist. "I about swallowed my tongue when I first saw you. All tanned muscles rippling all over the place. Then I caught wind of you…"

"I'd have put deodorant on if I knew a luscious siren was going to wash up on my beach that day." Jack smiled. He dipped his head to nibble her lips gently. "Ever since then, I couldn't seem to stop myself from showing up in your office every day."

"Come to think of it, you did pop in quite often. I thought it was because you were concerned I'd steal from you like the last coordinator did."

"I was."

Paige's mouth dropped open and she made to smack him, but he caught her hand and pressed kisses to her palm, trailing his lips up her arm, heat following the path of his lips.

"But I quickly realized," Jack continued, "That the only thing you were going to steal was my heart."

"Oh…" Paige breathed out as her heart did a weird little shiver in her chest and she tumbled head-first over the cliff into love.

"I've tried to push it away." Jack's lips were warm at her throat, his breath causing her to shudder, his hands stroking her back in a soothing motion. "You are my employee, after all."

"I am," Paige gasped as his hands found her breasts, and he gently thumbed her nipples into taut little peaks as he continued to speak.

"And so I tried being rude to you."

"Yes, I noticed. But that didn't last all that long." Paige's head dropped back as he continued to tease her breasts.

"And I tried to ignore the fact that you'd even bothered to give that idiot Horatio the time of day."

"Clearly a big mistake." She groaned as he bent and brought his mouth to her nipple, licking her through the fabric until it became moist and clung to her skin.

"And, I won't lie…I did take particular joy in always having to rescue that asshole. I hoped you would see that a real man would never turn off your power." With that Jack pulled her body against him and she gasped at the hard length that pressed into her stomach. Trailing his hand up her side and to her chin, he lifted her face so she was forced to look up at him.

Paige surprised herself by giggling at that.

"Maybe I'm not so poetic." Jack's smile flashed white in his tanned face. "But what I'm trying to say is he shaded your light. I would never wish that for you."

Caught on his words, Paige stretched up on her toes to wrap her arms around his neck.

"I don't need to be in the spotlight though. I don't… crave that."

"Not all lights need to be spotlights. You, my beautiful Paige, you just glow. You're like an ember in the fire that warms a room long after the flames have gone out. You soothe people. You bring comfort. You nurture. It's a gift you have."

"Jack…"

Jack bent his head and captured her lips, kissing her with an intensity that his other kisses had missed. This kiss…it was love, it was angst, and it held a quiet yearning for somebody to share their light with him. Paige fell into it, never wanting to let go, knowing that a life with him would be…perhaps not an easy one…but one in which she would never have to compromise who she was for the benefit of another.

Jack nudged her back toward the bed until her legs hit the mattress. He tugged the dress over her head, tossing it behind him, and she was left standing there in a simple pair of white panties.

"Sexy," Jack breathed. He ran his hand along the waistline of her panties, and little thrills of lust followed his touch. "I don't know why these turn me on so much."

"Really?" Paige laughed up at him.

"Oh yeah. *Very* puritan. And yet…I know you're not…" Paige gasped as he lifted her easily and pressed her back to the bed, splaying her legs open so he could trace his mouth along the edge of her underwear. A sigh escaped her as he kissed his way across her panties, finding the soft inner skin of her thighs, and she almost squirmed as his tongue traced lazy circles over the sensitive skin. Slowly, he peeled the cotton down her thighs, his mouth following its path, leaving Paige gasping for more. She didn't need all this. She wanted him inside her now.

"Jack…I need you. Now."

"In time, my love. In time. If you let me…we'll have all the time in the world."

Paige closed her eyes as the meaning of his words slipped through her, filling her with an almost unbearable yearning. She wanted this. To be loved equally by a partner who would never push her into the corner or try to overshadow her.

A hot flash of desire speared her core as Jack's mouth found her, licking deeply inside of her and causing her hips to jerk off the bed. He laughed, capturing her hips with both hands, and anchoring them as he began a torturous assault with his tongue. Slowly, as though he had nothing else in the world but time, Jack tasted her and teased her until a wave of lust washed over her so intensely she was surprised it didn't drown them both.

Pulling back, she wrenched her hips from Jack's hands, manic for him. Grabbing his arms, she pulled him to her, claiming his mouth with her own. Jack licked into her mouth, trying to slow her down, trying to soothe her – but panic built inside of Paige. It was as though she needed him to claim her – needed him to be inside her – so that she could know this was real.

Wrapping her legs around him, Paige angled herself just so. She groaned as he paused.

"Paige."

Paige opened her eyes and met his. In them she could see the vulnerability of the man who wanted to share the most intimate thing he had with her – his heart.

"Jack…I love you." For a moment, the words hung in the air and nerves shot through Paige. Perhaps it had been the wrong thing to say. Maybe it was too soon. But when relief washed over his face, Paige knew that by being vulnerable to him first, she'd given him the best gift of all.

She'd trusted him with her heart.

"I love you." It was a whisper at her lips, a wish sent into the eye of a storm, a blessing upon still waters. When he took her this time, her world shattered open and her path was chosen.

CHAPTER THIRTY-TWO

"Coffee." Paige croaked the words out as she rolled over and smashed her face into Jack's chest. Oh. He'd stayed.

"Ouch." Jack laughed. "You don't have to headbutt me, woman. I'll get you coffee."

A ridiculous pleasure shivered through her knowing that he'd stayed to be with her, instead of retreating to his cabin to hide their liaison from anyone.

"Let's both go. We should say goodbye to the guests anyway."

"I'll meet you in the reception hall then?" Jack had pulled himself from the bed, but then turned and pressed a lingering kiss to her lips. Giddiness slipped through Paige, and she smiled up at him as he dressed. He looked good in her bedroom, she decided. But then he looked good doing anything.

Oh yeah, she had it bad.

And there was certainly nothing wrong with that, Paige reminded herself as she showered and dressed. It was okay to be excited about a new relationship and to look forward to their future together. Sure, she'd been burnt before – but that didn't mean she couldn't ever trust herself near fire again. What a cold life it would be if that was the case.

Humming, Paige made her way to the reception hall. It was early still, the first rays of sunlight only just cresting over the ocean, and birds chattered happily as though a storm hadn't attacked the island days before. She drew up short when she saw CeCe and Whit standing by the bar with luggage at their feet. CeCe turned and assessed Paige as she approached.

It was the first time Paige had seen CeCe since the night of the storm and while she was still dressed impeccably, it was as though someone had switched CeCe's light off. Bruises marred the thin skin around her eyes, and her smile was slow to come.

"Good morning, gorgeous. You look well."

"Thank you." Paige couldn't exactly return the compliment. Stuck on what to say, Paige looked to Whit.

"Do you love him?" CeCe asked, and Paige's brows shot to her hairline as she looked at the other woman in shock.

"Do I…"

"Jack. You love him. Don't you?"

"I…" Paige searched CeCe's eyes and realized, for the first time, this was the mother talking. "Yes, I do. I know we've only known each other a short time. But I do."

CeCe waved her hand as though to brush that aside. "Time has no relevance in love. But it's what I needed to hear. I've so wanted this for him."

"What's going on here?" Paige breathed a little sigh of relief at Jack's voice behind her.

"Good morning, darling. You look…well." CeCe beamed at Jack, light coming into her eyes for the first time that morning.

"Why are your bags packed?" Jack, his hair still wet from his shower, looked between Whit and CeCe in confusion. A thundercloud passed over his face. "You're doing it again, aren't you? You're quitting here. Moving on to another project."

"I…" CeCe paused when Whit held up a hand and cut her off.

"Paige, I'd like to commend you for your excellent work on this past retreat. I understand that personal circumstances may have made it difficult for you, however I believe you conducted yourself with professionalism. I would like to offer you a full-time position here as the events coordinator and customer experience manager, along with a raise and full-time benefits."

"Wow," Paige breathed. "That's very kind of you."

"But why are your bags packed?" Jack interrupted, looking down at the luggage at their feet.

"It's time." CeCe stepped forward and grabbed Jack's hands. Looking up at him, a tremulous smile crossed her face.

"You're moving on to someplace else, aren't you? Just like you always do."

"No, Jack. Not this time. I'm going for help."

"You're…" Jack's mouth dropped open.

"Yes, Jack. My dearest boy. Whit has found a lovely rehabilitation center."

"For…" Jack couldn't seem to accept what his mother was trying to tell him.

"I'm going to try. I…I'm so sorry, Jack. I'm sorry I put your life at risk. I've been positively ashamed since the storm. It's time. I'm going to give this an honest go."

"I'm proud of you." Jack wrapped his arms around his mom and pulled her to him for a moment. Pulling back, CeCe reached up and patted his cheek.

"The time is right."

"Why now?" Jack asked.

CeCe stepped back and looked between Jack and Paige.

"I don't need to take care of you anymore." CeCe's meaning was clear as she held Paige's eyes and passed the baton of responsibility to her.

"Of me…" A confused look crossed Jack's face as he looked at CeCe and then followed her gaze to Paige. Understanding dawned. "You've been waiting until I found my person?"

"I don't want you to be alone. I may not have been the best mother, but I want you to know how much I've always loved you. It's time for me to step back."

"Mom." Jack pulled her in for another hug. "You don't have to worry about me. I'm okay."

"I'll always worry about you. But I'll worry less now. If Paige stays, that is."

Paige's heart twisted as the little family turned to look at her.

"Well, Paige? Do you accept the offer?" Whit asked, and Paige knew he spoke of more than the job position.

Paige paused as CeCe twisted her neck, her face still

pressed to Jack's chest, and met her eyes. Jack schooled his expression into nonchalance, but she could feel the tension radiating off him. Her eyes bounced to where Mariposa mopped the bar, carefully avoiding looking up, though Paige knew the bartender had heard everything. Luis walked out front, a machete swinging nonchalantly from his hand, and Martin's voice floated from the kitchen where he sang loudly with the radio.

Paige realized that in a short time, this motley crew of hotel staff had become her people. They were all a little weird, all a little broken, and all a little awesome in their own way. She didn't want to go back to her old life, oh no. These were her people and Tranquila Inn had quickly become home.

"I'd be honored to accept."

"That's a good girl. Come on then, love. We'll be late to the airport and you know I can't stand having to wait in line with all those tourists." Whit shuddered and picked up a suitcase.

CeCe came forward and surprised Paige by pulling her into a tight hug. "Take care of my boy. He may have hard edges, but his heart needs tending. You'll find no better man. I may have screwed up a lot of things in my life, but Jack is not one of them. I couldn't be prouder of the man I raised. You're lucky to have him."

"I'll take care of him, CeCe. I promise."

"I'll hold you to that." CeCe gave her a brisk nod and then stuck her nose in the air before trailing out to the dark-windowed sedan that had just pulled into the drive. Jack looked from her to the pile of luggage that she'd left for someone else to carry. Grinning, he shook his head, hefted the bags, and followed after her to load the trunk of the car.

"Here. You get a rum punch and one day off before you have to get ready for the next retreat." Mariposa pushed a tiki mug across the bar at Paige.

"Isn't it a little early?" Paige looked askance at the mug. She hadn't even had her coffee yet. Then her other words hit Paige.

"The next retreat?" Paige looked at Mariposa in horror as Jack returned to the bar and slid an arm casually around her shoulders.

"They arrive in three days. You didn't think a lil' storm like that would stop people from trying to get to paradise, did you?" Mariposa grinned at her.

"Little storm?" Paige's eyebrows went up.

"That was nothing...just wait until we get a category five."

Paige gulped her punch and met Jack's laughing eyes.

"Don't worry, sweets... just remember to take it poco poco. Everything will work itself out in the end..."

AFTERWORD

I had so much fun writing this book. I know that a lot of readers love my series, but once in a while I love to write stand-alone books because I have a story in my head that won't leave. This is one of those books. It really has been such a tough year globally, and I find myself gravitating toward light stories that help me escape to other worlds. I hope that this book provided you with an escape and that you were able to steal a few moments of calm as you enjoyed island life with Paige and Jack. And…just remember to take life poco poco when the going gets tough. Slow it down, take a deep breath, and try living life on island time for a little bit. You'd be surprised how much fades away when you do and you'll find that the things that matter get done and the things that don't? Well, they never much mattered at all. Sparkle on! -Tricia

Sign up for information on new releases, free books, and fun giveaways at my website www.triciaomalley.com

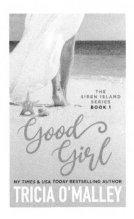

Not ready to leave Tricia O'Malley's tropical paradise? Then book another one way ticket to Siren Island! *Good Girl* calls to those who are ready to open their hearts, take risks, and believe in new beginnings - all on a seductive and magickal tropical Island.

The following is an excerpt from Good Girl

Book 1 in The Siren Island Series

CHAPTER 1

"Business or pleasure?"

"Business," Sam said automatically, her fingers tightening on the strap of the laptop case that rarely left her shoulder.

"And what is your business on Siren Island?" The customs agent spoke with a bouncy cadence, his words slow and richly rounded, the music of the islands flowing through his voice.

"I... I mean, pleasure," Sam said, startled to realize it was true. A drop of sweat slipped between her shoulder blades. That morning, in a haze of *what-the-hell-am-I-doing,* she'd donned what she'd come to term her Air Barbie uniform. It had breezed her through most airports in the world, straight into whatever hotel finance meetings she was attending, and had earned her more than her fair share of upgrades .

Impeccably tailored slacks? Check. Tasteful diamond stud earrings? Check. And a silk blouse in a muted color – not too bright, as she'd learned that the men in the board meetings she ran often took a power color as an invitation to flirt.

Though why she'd added her diaphanous silk scarf and patent leather sling-backs to the outfit, Sam had no clue.

Her plane wouldn't be landing in a fiercely air-conditioned airport with valets to whisk her luggage away as she went from one perfectly manicured space to the next. Oh no. Not even close.

Instead, here she was holding up a line of sweaty, boisterous passengers who all seemed to have overindulged on the plane ride down to whichever hotel's all-inclusive vacation package they'd signed up for. The sun, an angry unrepentant dictator, broiled them all with her cruel rays.

"Which is it, ma'am? Business or pleasure?" The customs agent regarded her carefully, and it annoyed Sam to see not even a sheen of sweat on the man's face, though he wore neatly pressed khaki pants and a button-down shirt. Why were there no enclosed rooms in this hut of an airport? Samantha knew for a fact that the island had access to the internet; surely they'd learned of the invention of air conditioning by now.

"Pleasure. My apologies. I travel so much for work that I forgot this trip was for pleasure," Sam said, sweeping her tastefully highlighted auburn hair over her shoulder and flashing the agent the smile that had opened more than one door for her in the past.

"That's a shame, ma'am. One should never forget to take time for pleasure." The agent's voice never changed, but something flashed in his eyes for just a moment – a warm male appreciation that, for once, didn't feel predatory. Sam got the impression that he enjoyed all women.

When she heard him begin flirting with the lady behind her, who sported a fanny pack and an unruly swath of grey hair, her assumption was confirmed.

His words followed her as she tapped her foot impatiently by the single-loop baggage conveyor belt, and Sam's annoyance reached peak levels as another passenger jostled her to peer over her shoulder.

"I really hope they didn't lose our bags this time. I swear, Carl, every time we come here something gets lost."

Then why did they still come here? Sam wondered in frustration, deliberately spreading her elbows a bit to strike a power pose – the one she used in crowds to force people to step away from her a bit.

For that matter, what was *she* even doing here? As Sam's thoughts flashed back over the last forty-eight hours, sweat began to drip in earnest down her back, and she was certain she could actually feel the blood pumping through her heart. Gulping for air, she looked around wildly. What this airport needed was some fans.

The sunlight seemed to get brighter and the eager laughter of the crowd around her sounded like the braying of mules. The faces and laughter and heat and sweat all pressed on her until Sam turned to run – only to find herself trapped by the crowd. Panic skittered its way up her throat and she gasped, trying to draw a breath against the warm press of bodies pushing toward the bags that now belched from a small flap-covered hole in the wall.

A hand closed on hers and Sam's gaze slammed into cool blue eyes – the color of the sea – and a calm wave of energy seemed to pour through her. She lost herself in the reassuring smile of a woman, a peaceful oasis of calm, who pulled her through the crowd.

"Sit." Samantha's butt had barely touched the seat when the woman unceremoniously pushed Sam's head between her legs. She gulped air, desperately trying to hold her panic attack at bay. The last thing she heard before it all went dark was the woman's voice.

"This one's mine."

Available now as an e-book, paperback or audiobook!

Available from Amazon

FINDING HAPPINESS IS THE BEST
REVENGE

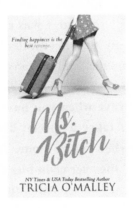

Also from Tricia O'Malley - Ms. Bitch
Read a free prequel chapter here!
https://www.triciaomalley.com/the-prequel
(No download required)

From the outside, it seems thirty-six-year-old Tess Campbell has it all. A happy marriage, a successful career as a novelist, and an exciting cross-country move ahead. Tess has always played by the rules and it seems like life is good. Except it's not. Life is a bitch. And suddenly so is Tess.

Read Today

"**Ms. Bitch is sunshine in a book! An uplifting story of fighting your way through heartbreak and making your own version of happily-ever-after.**"

~Ann Charles, USA Today Bestselling Author of the Deadwood Mystery Series

"**Authentic and relatable, Ms. Bitch packs an emotional punch. By the end, I was crying happy tears and ready to pack my bags in search of my best life.**"

-Annabel Chase, author of the Starry Hollow Witches

"**It's easy to be brave when you have a lot of support in your life, but it takes a special kind of courage to forge a new path when you're alone. Tess is the heroine I hope I'll be if my life ever crumbles down around me. Ms. Bitch is a journey of determination, a study in self-love, and a hope for second chances.**"

-Renee George, USA Today Bestselling Author of the Nora Black Midlife Psychic Mysteries

"**I don't know where to start listing all the reasons why you should read this book. It's empowering. It's fierce. It's about loving yourself enough to build the life you want. It was honest, and raw, and real and I just...loved it so much!**"

– Sara Wylde, author of Fat

"Love her books and was excited for a totally new and different one! Once again, she did NOT disappoint! Magical in multiple ways and on multiple levels. Her writing style, while similar to that of Nora Roberts, kicks it up a notch!! I want to visit that island, stay in the B&B and meet the gals who run it! The characters are THAT real!!!"

- Amazon Review -

THE MYSTIC COVE SERIES

ALSO BY TRICIA O'MALLEY

Wild Irish Heart

Wild Irish Eyes

Wild Irish Soul

Wild Irish Rebel

Wild Irish Roots: Margaret & Sean

Wild Irish Witch

Wild Irish Grace

Wild Irish Dreamer

Wild Irish Christmas (Novella)

Wild Irish Sage

Wild Irish Renegade

———

Available in audio, e-book & paperback!

"I have read thousands of books and a fair percentage have been romances. Until I read Wild Irish Heart, I never had a book actually make me believe in love." - Amazon Review -

---

Available in audio, e-book & paperback!

"Not my usual genre but couldn't resist the Florida Keys setting. I was hooked from the first page. A fun read with just the right amount of crazy! Will definitely follow this series."

- Amazon Review -

THE ISLE OF DESTINY SERIES

ALSO BY TRICIA O'MALLEY

Stone Song

Sword Song

Spear Song

Sphere Song

Available in audio, e-book & paperback!

"Love this series. I will read this multiple times. Keeps you on the edge of your seat. It has action, excitement and romance all in one series."

- Amazon Review -

ACKNOWLEDGMENTS

First, and foremost, my friends for their constant support, advice, and ideas. You've all proven to make a difference on my path. And, to my beta readers, I love you for all of your support and fascinating feedback!

And last, but never least, my two constant companions as I struggle through words on my computer each day - Briggs and Blue.

Thanks for reading my story that I so lovingly put out into the world. I hope it brought you light and joy! If you can, I'd be honored if you left a review. A book can live and die by reviews and I so very much want my book to live. (Please don't kill my book!)

Oh, and if you're into island and puppy photos – you can find me on Facebook and Instagram.